Betty May

My First Life

by

Melvyn Lumb

1

Cover Illustration:

Young Woman with a Fan by Pietro Rotari

To, Margaret, Lynda and Nigel.

My thanks, they have helped me in different ways.

My thanks also to Stuart, Donald and all the members of The Jersey (CI) Writers Social Group. Without their help and encouragement this book would never have been published.

Contents

Chapter One: Worsthorne Abbey

Born a bastard in the winter of the year of our Lord 1723, I started this diary as an eleven-year-old and as soon as I learned to write to a fair degree, (all with the kind help of Sister Nichols).

I wrote with my dear Mother's memory in mind. Oh! How I missed her over the years, and do but wonder why these pages be not stained by my tears. My early life contained some happiness, though due to our poor circumstances' heartache was never far away. For some reason only known to God, I had always been proud of my name, 'Betty May,' taken from my mother's name. Times for me have by good fortune and hard work changed to some degree. So strange as my story be, I most humbly believe it to be worthy of a reading.

We join the story as I, at the age of thirteen, leave Worsthorne Abbey where I was looked after for the previous four years, and taught to read and write by the good Sisters. Sister Bernadette, is about to escort me the five miles to my first paid position of pantry maid at Colesdale Hall. By this date my Dear Mother had died from consumption.

11th May, the year of our Lord 1736.

My entry into the Abbey as a frightened young child so long ago, took me up the six front steps and through those same huge oak doors, this day I leave behind. Now I could read and write to some fair degree and a much more advantaged girl now, did I feel. Never did the fact that I be a bastard ever leave my mind. This changed me not, with the comparison of my younger self those years past.

I had all I owned (which included my precious diary) packed inside a small bundle and tied with string in such fashion as to afford me with a means to carry it. So, with it over my shoulder, we set off in the early morn, on the near five-mile journey. I remember it was windy and bright with sunshine. I often stopped as my wont, to observe, and enjoy the scent of wild flowers and anything else that caught my eye. Sister Bernadette forbade me to waste time or pick any flowers. She had much trouble at times with her habit and garb in the wind, as her hands battled to keep it all in place. To keep me walking and distracted was her intention, as she tried to speak to me with a never tiring tongue. Her hope and indeed effort, I am afraid, only partly worked. My youthful years made me respond with such gaiety and energy that I diverged on the occasion from our path. At one point I noticed a small spread of forget-me-nots next to a patch of purple heather.

'Please, Sister Bernadette, may I pick a small posy for myself and one for you?'

'Yes, you may, but only one for yourself. We have miles yet to go.'

I wasted no time and soon had a few of these beautiful flowers to pin to my apron. My stop took me but a minute and nothing was said. Soon we were on our way again. The talk started again with our walk and did again continue like afore. I only but half listened to her discourse, I am ashamed to say, for my interest was taken by the beautiful scents from the flowers.

'Oh, I do but love the sweet scent, if I could only carry it in a bottle.'

'They so suit you. Forget-me-nots go well with your eyes.'

I am taken a little by surprise, 'Blue?. . . My eyes?'

I never took any notice before and tis true to say that we had no looking glass in the Abbey. (The Sisters discouraged vanity.)

'Yes, and pretty too.' she added thoughtfully.

I remember being a little shocked. My mother may have called my eyes pretty as a small child. I had no memory of this. At the time for some reason, I believed that as a bastard I must surely be ugly.

'The boys will be at pains... not to remark about them. You must be careful... and keep your virtue.' She stopped for a moment to catch her breath.

This came out while we laboured up a steep incline, as we followed the ancient Roman merchant's trail over the moor.

'I've no inclination to follow my mother's fate. Though I loved her as well as any daughter could.'

Dear sister Bernadette looked at me and nodded.

I had nothing and a thousand things all to ask her. The realisation struck me like a blow delivered by a stave, this would be the last time I would have a chance to speak to her. I felt hollow inside. What if no one likes me? I worry my time away as we walk. Enough had been told me about where I was to start work and how I was to behave. Those times beyond counting I had to repeat, 'Do not speak unless spoken to, and try not to shout your answers!'

Even at my young age I understood what be required of me. Despite this, I felt a fair need for someone to watch and guide me. What I didn't fully realise at this time be how a mouth like mine could get me into trouble. I believe that I may follow my mother in that respect.

The journey took us forever as we climbed up over countless rocky fells and down into shallow valleys. We passed a small lake which rested in a lower region skirted by steep hills. Then I felt my heart leap as only a young girls could, when Sister Bernadette pointed to a huge house in the distance, around which nestled several smaller buildings. The area was covered in an abundance of trees.

I stopped to gaze at a house so grand, that never had I seen the likes of before, nor dreamed of entering. This was Colesdale Hall. Eventually we arrived at the servant's door. She kept a firm hold of my hand, lest I develop any idea of running away. I found that strange, for where could I run? While she knocked with that rusty brown thing on that huge green door, a continued tight grip was kept of my hand. It was beyond my reasoning for I had not one idea of running. I would never run away, for I know it to be God's will, and my duty to obey and trust the Sisters. Although life had been hard at the Abbey over the years, the Sisters were fair and I had been treated as befitted my status in the eyes of the Lord. This left me with some idea of my lowly station and how I would be treated in my employment. I knew well how to behave as a thirteen-year-old bastard girl. It had been drummed into me over time, along with a good education.

So, I waited patiently, watched over by this dear Sister Bernadette whom, as circumstances had dictated, I freely regarded as my second mother. Growing for some uncountable reason fearful at the last moment of my future as planned by God, I found despite my earlier fortitude, I be now short of this previous strength and sadly reluctant to leave her. I believe I did whimper so. Sister Bernadette was kind to me as she described this household so full of good people. She was almost right in what she told me. I often wondered about her over the years, if she still be in good health, and a devoted nun.

'Now Betty, you have been with us in God's house for four years now, and I want you to promise me that you will keep up with your prayers. You have much to thank him for and I know that you are an honest child, but you must watch that tongue of yours and learn to hold it.' Sister Bernadette gave me a kindly look and a wink.

I for my part held on tightly to my little bundle of pathetic possessions, so precious were they. We waited for a long time, until a woman of not unkind countenance and generous proportions opened the big green door.

'Come this way,' she said, all full of airs as she stood back and wiped flour off her hands onto her apron.

As we entered the kitchen, the sweet smell of baking assailed my senses and I remember how my mouth watered so. And to the same degree my imagination did wonder about who ate all this fine food, for I knew that this would not be mine to taste. I was soon to be brought back to earth and my childish thoughts forgotten as I looked up at this well boned woman who stood afore me. I noticed a few of her brown curls had escaped from under the lace front of her cook's head covering. This be at odds with her otherwise neat appearance. She sounded gruff at first. Perhaps she disliked me, for I knew I must have presented a fair sight in my threadbare pinafore and old shoes given to me by the nuns.

'And your name, young girl?'

She spent no small time looking at me up and down, while she waited for me to answer. I fear I may have been occupied with my own thoughts, for Sister Bernadette broke the silence between us.

'This be Betty May, a bright young girl of thirteen years, who can read and write... well.'

'I am Fanny Grimshaw; Miss Grimshaw to you. You will be working for me in the kitchen.'

'Master Jenkins, the head of the household staff, will be here in a minute to see to you.'

She turned her back on us and walked away to tend her boiling pans.

Now I trembled so, and my belly felt unwell. Her words had struck me in a way which gave me no pleasure, for I had become used to working with the sisters and saw few men or boys close to, over the years. So now 'a man' was to be the head over me.

Then from nowhere, although I realised that people do not come from nowhere, a tall man dressed in a black jacket and starched white shirt came with speed towards us. I stood in no small fear and discomfort, for if it be possible, I would dearly have liked to disappear and been elsewhere - anywhere in fact. For I perceived a sour look of displeasure upon his face, sourer than any crab apple. This did cause me to worry that I be the source of his unpleasant countenance. The owner of this face be Master Jenkins.

'Oh, my words, what have you brought me here - a young child? I need a lass that can do a day's work.'

This tall, black-haired man looked down upon my miserable self, then shrugged his shoulders and shook his head. Overcome with much unease, and with my heart racing away, I considered myself unfairly judged. I knew I be of at least normal height and, although light of build, I believed I showed only good health and no sign of disease.

'And what age is this waif may I ask you Sister. . . erm?'

'Bernadette, Sister Bernadette. . . Betty May, as you see (she motioned towards me with her hand) is all of thirteen years, a good worker and well educated for her class.'

'Ha! Ha! An education! She will need it all right, scrubbing pots and pans.' An evil grin slid over his face.

I stood before him like a statue. His hands checked me from top to toe, and took his time in certain areas. Then he scribed a circle in the air with his fore finger. I turned around. I shrank with fear as he felt my arms and legs for muscles and then another area. I liked that not.

'This child is nothing but skin and bone, there is little flesh or muscle.'

'It be her age. She has grown apace, I think you will agree that she is quite tall for her age,' said Sister Bernadette.

'Open your mouth,' he ordered.

My uncomfortable, nay fearful heart filled me with indecision and I moved not.

'Show me your teeth you silly girl!' (He shoved his dirty finger into my mouth to move my lips for a better look). Hum! Not bad, you do clean them occasionally, don't you?'

'Yes sir. Argh!' I could not help but splutter, so foul be the taste in my mouth. To be touched again by this stranger, the very thought made me tremble so.

'I use a cotton cloth with salt every day, as the good Sisters did show me.' I felt inclined to say little else.

'I be addressed as Master Jenkins. Only the head of the house is referred to as Mam and as most unusually, there is no lady in charge of this house, so Sir John is the head and always called Sir. Is that understood?'

I took my time and nodded. With that, Master Jenkins' inspection of me came to a thankful end. I fear I would have refused to allow his finger anywhere near my mouth again. Nor to touch me anywhere; this could have caused no end of strife for my poor self; I had after all seen horses at York market inspected in much the same way. And with all that be true, may God be my witness, with far more humanity too. This I do believe. Our once-a-year trip organised by the nuns was a highlight in my life, something we all looked forward to and I will sorely miss.

'Well, we will see if you can do the work correctly. You will be sent back if you cannot!'

Every word I did believe and worried so. For in truth and beyond what the sisters indicated, I had no true idea what to expect. I suffered no small melancholy with the memory that Sister Bernadette left me at this time to my fate. I fear my childlike dismay was there for all to see. I remember it well as I sought to wrap my arms around her, my head buried in the folds of her habit. She held me for a brief time and said these few words which I still remember:

'Now Betty, remember what you have learned from the Sisters. And always say your prayers. You know that you can return, should you choose to be a Sister at Worsthorne Abbey! Don't leave it too long though,' her voice faltered.

All too soon her time came to leave. And I remember the kindness of Miss Grimshaw, which filled me with some hope for the future, and had a certain calming effect upon my soul, when she said, "I've laid out some roast pork, cheese and bread for you Sister Bernadette and I'll not see you leave without a cup of our home-made cider." With that she poured a generous measure from the stone jug into a wooden cup for her fortification on the long walk back. Soon the Sister had left me with but a wave as she walked down the path.

Master Jenkins spoke to Miss Grimshaw, within my hearing, which I liked not.

'The waif's as poor as a jail-house mouse. I can hardly believe she reads and writes. What is happening in the world these days, I ask you?'

Miss Grimshaw agreed, 'Yes well, this is the most we can expect with her background, a bastard and all. We be soon to find out if she can work to rules.'

'Yes, to my rules. That be the important part of the matter!' He looked disinterested as he picked his teeth with a thumb nail.

I had to listen to all this spoken in front of me. . .though I had no businesses to make a remark, I still be sorely tempted; at another time I surely would have.

'You come with me now, and bring your bundle?' He curled his first finger as an indication for me to follow. He felt it fit to have no name to call me at the time. I had names for him which would do me no good if I uttered them aloud. I made a mental note to watch my mouth in more relaxed times.

So, I nodded and off he charged. I had to hurry to keep up with him. My stupid worry that he would round a corner and be gone when I got there was unfounded though, to be true, he had no shrift with me at this stage. We climbed two staircases and walked in semi-darkness down to the end of a long dank corridor. Before me stood a tall ladder that seemed to disappear out of sight into a dark void, so high did it go.

'Up there wench be where you will sleep.'

'Such monsters I do espy, I couldn't for the love of the Lord sleep in such a place, I beseech you Master Jenkins.'

This was the last time I foolishly allowed myself to show such emotions and indeed weakness. For the great delight in Master Jenkins' laugh did somehow sicken my belly.

'Do not be silly wench, for there be very few mice now since the cat had been locked up there. Perhaps you would rather repose in the barn, for I could arrange it?'

I did shiver at the thought.

'What are you waiting for? Take your bundle up there at once. I do not have all day.'

With great reluctance and fear, I climbed that ladder rung by rung with my bundle in one hand. Hardly had my eyes become used to the darkness when I heard my name called. I hurried and, on the way back to the kitchen, Master Jenkins showed me the fires that had to be lit every morning before dawn, and where the coal and firewood and matches were kept.

Minutes later I stood in a corner of the kitchen where Master Jenkins left me; I stayed as quiet as the mice which I'd been convinced would share my bed. But this was no time to relax, for I could only wonder at what awaited me. I blinked to make sure I had seen true, because there at the other end of the table stood a girl; I later learned she be only one year older than me. She looked at me and smiled. I for my part smiled back and nodded.

'I be Sarah the chamber maid. I also help in the kitchen when my duties upstairs are completed. There's only Sir John to look after. So that leaves me free of work at times,' she spoke.

'And I'm Betty May,' I nodded again.

It was at this moment that Miss Grimshaw entered the kitchen and noticed me.

'Come here child. I would guess you be hungry?'

'Yes Miss Grimshaw.'

On second look, she still seemed to me to be a lady of stern countenance, and at first did little to make me feel at ease, though to be true I had seen her act to the contrary. A steaming half pint mug of cabbage water was given to me with a crust of bread, slathered in beef dripping, and but little cheese. This did revive me. I for once had no desire to converse with anyone. I realised that tears still lay just below the surface.

My duties were light for the rest of the day. This was followed by a fitful night's sleep. All sorts of monsters I did imagine as I hid my head under the coverlet. It be a small comfort when I found out that a skylight gave a good shaft of light during the day. This I hesitated to call a bedroom. To be honest, as I was taught by my mother, I never in my life had what could be called a bedroom to myself. I slept in a dormitory, so I by the Grace of God and the rules of the house did accept my humble but singular sleeping chamber.

I remember well the first morn, as a grumpy Miss Grimshaw dragged me out of bed more asleep than awake. This was accompanied by dire warnings about the perils of not rising on time in future.

I understood from the start that she loathed climbing that ladder. It's not hard to imagine her ample frame, and her difficulty in arriving safely at the place where my bed lay. This be daybreak, I believed about five of the clock and a time for further instruction. We started with the range in the kitchen and the way to carry two buckets at once to save time. I found this to be hard until I became used to it.

'Now we must rake out the ashes like this and remove them with the black metal shovel into this bucket. Then you lay the fire, light it and place the coal on the burning wood, carefully using these pincers.'

I am expected to do this every morn including Sundays.

'This be the place where the scullery maid eats. You wear this pinafore and it be expected to last you for a week. Do not soil it whatever you do.'

I peered through the open door into the small larder with relief, as I spotted a large sack of dried peas that would fashion as a seat. With just a slice of bread and either a piece of cheese or meat to eat, I had no need for a table.

I decided from the start to take a serious note of anything that Miss Grimshaw said to me.

Master Jenkins presented himself as quite another matter. Even at this early stage I felt by instinct a certain disquiet, or was it fear for this man? I beheld his actions to be of no benefit nor care for me. I wanted not to be near him. Oh, how I would like him to feel the rough edge of my tongue. I knew at my young age I must keep a hold of it for now.

My hours were long and although I tried not to, I did have cause to rest my eyes more than once. The power of sleep occasionally enticed me to a state which filled me with shame. Once, when nearly caught by Master Jenkins, in my memory I told no lies, nor would I ever, had I been questioned about my sinful state.

Well used to the plain but adequate food at the nunnery, I

found it difficult at first to become used to the small amount provided me in my new position. This gave me a hunger for more food as I so needed, and I started to pick at certain food scraps, I be most ashamed to say from plates of beef, almost untouched food laid out, and not used at breakfast time. I did ask in my prayers for forgiveness for my sins of theft, as I tried to be a better person.

Early December, the year of our Lord 1736.

For about six months I laboured hard. It had always been a point of pride that I worked to my best ability. I believed I might follow my mother in this respect. It was lonely for a young girl such as I, by myself in an attic room with only the Lord as an absent companion. I called him thus, for where did he hide? Not one sign, not one word of comfort, or answer to my many prayers. There! I've started again. Perhaps it be just as well I talk to my diary about such things as only my pen can witness.

It would seem to me that my work be passed as fair to middling. Great temptations presented themselves to open my mouth and talk back, especially with my concern for Master Jenkins and his dislike for me, for which I cared not. I remembered the Nuns' instructions to keep a fair reign on my tongue. For, if truth be told, I gave little reason for his carping and regular criticism of my work.

    Miss Grimshaw, by all truthful recounts, shares some part of my views. I take something of a liberty to describe her thus and it be only for the sake of propriety, in my diary. I did feel a certain softening of her attitude towards me around the kitchen which be her domain. And in all modesty, I tried my best to work hard, and often had the chance, and pleasure to do more than expected of me. A curious warm feeling of pride did I feel, if my small efforts made it a little easier for her. Perhaps she realised that I had become useful to her in the work. Besides, by this time I had become a little fond of her.

Chapter Two: Jess the Cocker Spaniel

My first true friend with some surprise be Master Jenkins dog Jess. It be true that Miss Grimshaw, be the first to notice something in the way Jess behaved.

'Betty, I do believe that Jess has taken to you,' she said. 'I can't be surprised because of the cruel way Master Jenkins treats her. And how well you look after her when little more than a young maid yourself. I be sure these creatures understand more than we think.'

'I cannot even think of causing harm to any creature,' I said, 'nor seeing the harm done to a small mite like Jess.'

Miss Grimshaw was in a prattling mood (which may be most of the time) as she introduced me to certain facts regarding Jess, 'Did you know that Jess was given to Sir John by the rector as thanks for some favour he granted the parish. He said he wanted to be helpful because the litter of thirteen had been too many for the parish to use. Sir John had a notion to try and train Jess to hunt the woodcocks in nearby Hurstwood, it being a bird he be most partial to, and cocker spaniels be bred for this purpose.'

I was to but find out much later that Sir John had been offered four spaniels. A picture of his dead wife painted some years before with her favourite spaniel did perchance stir such memories which still haunt and upset him occasionally. This be the reason why he would only accept just the one. It was only then did I realise why he gave the dog to Master Jenkins as a gift. It be to keep her in the house ready when required, only for the purpose of an occasional hunt and not as a constant reminder of his deceased wife, Marie.

So, this was why I be expected to look after the dog's feeding and walking on days when she wasn't required for the hunt. Jess would on the occasion require a good scrub. I had seen Master Jenkins at such times wash her down in a rough fashion with cold water and horse soap, by the well. She hated this and would mysteriously disappear at the first sign of the appearance of the washing bucket from the stables. Master Jenkins generally ended up in a foul temper by the time Jess had been caught. This inflammation of temper would cause him to take it out on her with a stick. At this time, I be a young pantry maid of only a few months experience that a good wind would blow over. Despite this, it be impossible for me to stand idle, for I couldn't bear to hear Jess scream so and for so long. It was against my character to ignore poor Jess's plight.

Because of this I usually showed myself to him so he knew I watched his behaviour, though to be truthful I cannot say he changed much because of me. I would on occasion shout to him.

'You be nothing but a bully Master Jenkins,' or the like, 'Pick on someone your own size.' there were other choice calls I made to him. One or two I won't repeat. To this he would usually shout something like, "Go back to your work, WAIF,' This would be accompanied by a warning.

On one occasion he chased me with the stick. This would have been dangerous, had he caught me. He be one to soon work himself into a frenzy, to such heights, and spitting froth around his mouth. So, I made use of the light weight of my frame which made me quick of foot. Once he chased me into the kitchen where the cook Miss Grimshaw worked. Fortunately for me, the sight of her working there, calmed Master Jenkins enough to afford me a far from certain degree of safety.

From that first day and onwards I always had a warm place in my heart for Jess, especially later when I truly found out about the friendship, and constant love a dog holds for the lucky person it regards as its master.

Then something happened to me that started a change in my life. I would rather it hadn't occurred the way it did. That day there blew a bitter, cruel wind from the North. Heavy rain clouds cruised our way like the large merchant ships I had seen in the master's paintings. This December day, the year of our

Lord 1736, was a day I would like to forget.

It started in a tired way; I was disadvantaged as I'm about to explain. On my mind there be all that Miss Grimshaw required of me and this weighed heavily upon me. Today she be baking bread and pies, as well as roasting a large joint of pork. So, with this in mind, my first work in the morn be to light the big kitchen oven. This must be made ready and at baking temperature by six of the clock, in time for her to start work. My evening would again be spent cleaning, and making some preparation for breakfast the following day. I knew I would have to toil until eight of the clock.

My chores this morn were normal as such. Perhaps I be a little slower than usual to wake up; sleep most days seemed to hang over me like a cloud: perchance not my best part of the day. Five of the clock would see me sometimes stumble or be a little clumsy of foot; today more than usual. I knew I must use the ladder with all care, while sleep gripped its weary claws into my brain. A little time would pass each morn afore I became part of the world I so diligently worked for. I always tried to be quiet as I cleaned out and lit the five fires around the house. I also had to be careful because during one of these chores two days ago I by accident spilled a little ash down the front of my pinafore, which left a black mark I couldn't remove. This brought the wrath of Master Jenkins down upon me. He was in a good mood and only warned me severely against any more misdoings, so I was not beaten.

Chapter Three: A dog's dinner

Yesterday evening our Jess had caught six woodcocks. It was my work to pluck the freshly caught birds, and prepare them so the cook could bake the woodcock pie for Sunday lunch. This was my last chore in the evening; I had to leave the birds hung up in the larder from an old washing line. By the time I cleared all the feathers and tidied up I was almost asleep on my feet. Tis true my hunger couldn't quell my need for sleep, even though yesterday I had my meagre ration of bread and cheese. Not a morsel of extra food had passed my lips, and today I had yet to eat.

This morn I entered the kitchen at five of the clock. My tired eyes barely opened, so tired did I feel, my weak knees made me unsteady upon my feet. My empty belly rumbled like distant thunder. To add to my woes, I faced a long hard day of toil.

As I approached the pantry, I noticed the door ajar. Something was wrong. I peered in and before me there spread a sight of utter carnage. Unable to understand at first, I did rub my eyes to try and convince myself I was mistaken, and that somehow, I still slept.

'Oh no! God help me. . . no!' I whimpered.

Scattered everywhere, bits and pieces of dried bone and gore covered the floor, stuck to the walls, the table, and any place else within range, of an active, and ever hungry spaniel. Because of my selfish thoughts for myself, I must have pulled the larder door shut and forgotten to close the latch. This allowed Jess to somehow open the door and plunder Sir's birds. Every bird had been chewed to pieces. How she managed to reach them, at first I could only guess.

She lay in the corner in her basket with a rather contented look about her. At first, I be stunned by the sight, then I finally worked out that she must have somehow jumped up onto the table and stood on her hind legs to reach the woodcocks.

'Oh Jess! How could you do this to me?' I moaned. My head spun. I took a deep breath and felt no better. 'My dear Lord. . .what can I do I now?' I muttered. I fell to my knees and wretched up a little liquid, I had no food to part with. My wet hands covered my face and tears streamed down my arms.

'Jess, you're a bad, bad dog!'

She watched me out of those large brown intelligent eyes, which now had a distinctly guilty look.

Unable to think, I remained there for I know not how long. My shaky wet hands still engulfed my face. With the will of God, I would rather kneel here forever. Or a better idea crossed my mind, if the world could just split open and cause me to disappear. . . 'Oh no,' I whispered at the thought. Trouble awaited me, and would come soon enough. Jess came to me and licked my face; I knew she could tell I be distressed.

At last, I gathered together any wits I had left. And with water, bucket, scrubbing brush and rag, I set to work and cleaned up as best I could. This took an hour's toil and two buckets of water, carried from the well. Although I be able to remove most of the terrible gore, there be stains left on the floor, and as for the wall, well, only more white wash would cover up my sin.

'I'm for it now,' I moaned to myself again, and rushed to see to the fires.

At work and unable to concentrate I was but a trembling wreck, as I awaited my fate. Then my blood ran cold as I heard 'BETTY!' This be Master Jenkins, who screamed out for all in England to hear and tremble therefore. I knew from whence it came, and I ran as if a lamb to slaughter. Down the cold stone stairs, I slowed to a gingerly pace, and entered the kitchen one step at a time, with much upset in my belly. I stopped and chanced a look.

Chapter four: My Punishment

Master Jenkins charged up to me as one who be well on the way to madness, with face aglow, and arms folded. As always when annoyed, he seemed to tower even higher above me than before, I felt drawn to look up, and met his evil glare which penetrated like a devil's curse. I have but little recollection of how I acted, so overcome with dire feelings be I.

I was struck by the red face of a concerned Miss Grimshaw.

'I see you have fed the Sir's food to my dog. This will have to be punished, I must see to that. A terrible crime you saw fit to allow,' His eyes changed, and he boiled liked a pot of oil into a spitting rage.

Master Jenkins turned away and mumbled something in temper, as his right foot swung back and then stabbed out in vicious fashion, I could not but imagine such savagery had I not seen it for myself; the force hit Jess on her hind quarters and, be such as to hurl the poor animal against the wall with considerable force. She screamed out in pain and surprise. Her loud yelping did pierce my soul to no small degree. I was sure she be hurt, by the way she continued to yelp.

Without thought for myself I turned to her, dropped to my knees and, petted her for but a minute. She now whimpered so at the ministration of Master Jenkins. Her large sad spaniel eyes bore into mine and I saw the hurt and a flash of something, was it thanks, relief that someone cared, or was it perhaps love, just for me?

So sorry did I feel for her, an animal. I felt sure at that moment she knew; by the guilty look which flowed across her features. Who had the worst circumstance at this time, I be not sure. Master Jenkins uttered something as he approached me. His powerful fist came into heavy, painful contact with the side of my head. Stars shone behind my eyes, then blackness befell me like a dark velvet hood.

I returned to the world somewhat fuzzy of head, and climbed to my feet in an unsteady, shaky manner. I held back tears that I had no wish to show this horrible man. But almost beyond my powers to stop. I shook with fear, and knew I deserved all I got. My head throbbed. What more do I have to endure now, I wondered? Some of these memories I describe were not easy to recall due to my poor condition at the time.

'I warned you, and you did this,' Master Jenkin's clenched fist punched painfully at my shoulder in temper. 'You will not do this again!' he spat out, his voice loud, yet breathless with rage. His glaring eyes like flaming black candles were a worry for me.

'It has been brought to my attention that the dog's dinner be still in its bowl untouched. Now we can't have any waste, can we?' A small drool dripped from to his ugly chin onto his black top coat collar where it formed an obscene, white puddle.

I felt this man's large rough hand grab the top of my slender arm. So here, by all that be bad, his temper again disadvantaged me, and he cruelly dragged me outside into that chilled December weather and across the yard. I bore bruises, and painful swelling in my right shoulder the next day.

He did cast me forth onto the rough, flag-covered yard. T'was there I skinned my knees.

Then he made me sit on the icy cold and damp stone flags. Before I understood his intentions, he had fitted around my neck a dog collar with a short chain. This he secured by some means to the wall. A nearly full dog's bowl he pushed afore me with his foot. Twas with much horror I realised his intention.

'I'll not see any more waste,' he sneered, 'You will stay here until you have eaten all the dog's food, and apologised for this terrible deed.'

I did but glance towards the bowl with my eyes almost shut. I had as little desire to picture the contents as indeed to eat this fare. I could imagine the contents of the dog bowl and that be enough for now.

'You're lucky there wasn't a bone in there,' he added as he walked away.

Never in my life had I heard of such a thing. I was thirteen and a half years old and always hungry. But I would rather starve than eat this. Meanwhile my stomach churned at the thought of the dog having eaten part of the food.

I had been there only a few minutes and already frozen stiff with cold, I shivered so. My thin pinafore dress and petticoat were all I had to wear; without the benefit of even a mean shawl to cover my shoulders. Indeed, it would be my good fortune to own one. The dull light showed poor weather soon to be upon us. I worried so where this might lead. My shivering had some affect upon my mind, I'm sure. Would I live to see the morrow, or be some waif who died through lack of homely shelter? I looked about me. There was nowhere to cast the dog food. My spirits dropped to almost desperate levels.

I sobbed my heart out and cried 'Oh, Dear Lord, please help a poor, worthless soul such as I.'

It was then when my body started to shake with no little violence. This scared me enough to know that I must do something in haste, so I shouted out, 'Master Jenkins, please forgive me!' which of course went unheard.

In pure desperation I decided to do the unthinkable. I looked reluctantly into that bowl, 'of things' - green, white, brown, of fat and vile stuff stuck together. My belly threatened me. Should I?

I called for God's mercy again. I wished that he should see me with this chain so short, 'Is he happy with my plight?' I asked myself. I did so wonder at first why a "perfect" being could be so heartless. Yet he still chose to ignore me. 'Where are you, Lord?'

I had to sit back on those stone flags. I knew there be nowhere to throw the food, nor hide it in this large back yard. So, must I try to eat some? I could feel my arms quiver with enough violence to shake my body. With some difficulty I held my nose to perchance hide the loathsome smell and, a little of the taste. Between shaky fingers, I lifted some of this slimy mess into my mouth. So revolting was it, I had to spit it back into the bowl. Unable was I to clear my mouth despite trying to spit it all out. I could only try to gag. There was nothing more to bring up.

I took a deep breath; I must try again. My fingers shook as I pushed some more of the slimy mess into my mouth. Pushing, pushing it in, as if ravenously hungry, I forced myself to try and swallow without having even chewed it. I tried in my desperation not to taste that vile smelling, horrible mess. It was the hardest thing I'd ever done in my life. I managed to keep down the first part mouthful. The second was another matter, as the taste became too much for me. My stomach revolted and I retched violently.

I felt now as if in a hell on earth. I tried to stop myself, only to retch again, unable to stop, with the taste still with me. I wretched in such desperation as never I want to do again. I shook uncontrollably and it was then I started to cry out and moan with frozen exhaustion.

'Oh, my dear Lord, I beseech you! Please help me. Stop me from being this stupid miserable wretch that I be.'

A bitter wind blew across the yard, and I shivered cruelly. This was hard to bear, sat out in the freezing backyard.

Then it began to rain upon my poor body. Soon the water soaked through my petticoats down to my skin. Now I be cold as never before in my short life. My teeth chattered hard as if to break. Chilled to the bone, I knew not how this would end. What next? Did I truly deserve all this? In trouble now, I knew it would not be long before I swooned. What depth of misery would I have to endure before my release? My distress may be imagined as I feared for the worst. My cries became desperate. To survive was my only goal. It was then that I believe I started to scream.

The rain only lashed me harder as if in punishment. Somewhere deep within me I took this to be a message from God. He didn't care about my poor soul. I remembered this more than anything else.

'Someone please . . . please!'

Scared for my worthless fate, I sobbed my heart out. I feared my tears and screams were washed away by the flood of ice-cold rain. Never had I felt so wretched, so forgotten and so frozen. Numbness began to spread throughout my body as the icy water flowed under my clothing. I had no idea what dreadful sounds I made in my anguish, for I started to feel warm. In spite of this I know I screamed out, for what little sense there remained warned me of my awful state. I became drowsy. I have an idea I remained so for far too long a time in my desperate state. I remember the sorrow I felt for what I had done. I was told all this and more, and know little about how long I sobbed and screamed out loud. And I may have called out to the Lord again for his mercy. My memories are few and hazy of this terrible time.

Master Jenkins had by now calmed down (with a small glass of Sir John's port). And returned to the kitchen, as he quietly shut the cellar door, he stopped to listen.

'What was that?' he said under his breath, as he heard a feint and high-pitched sound.

'That sounds like. . . Oh Jesus!' he remembered Betty May in the yard.

Miss Grimshaw heard nothing as she stoked the kitchen fire.

He dashed out into the backyard.

I have but a hazy memory of Master Jenkins who appeared.

He looked down at me. Said something. And, took off the dog collar from around my neck. I lay there on that chilled flagstone floor, my trembling form, now like cold butchers meat, and rain drenched. At last, I'm rescued. I think he tried to calm me. And I felt some small relief.

But then he left me. . . I fear I be beyond any consoling at this stage. I believe my plight, my desperate spirit, did cause me to shout and perhaps scream out again. I had no idea that true rescue was but minutes away. And the reason for Master Jenkins hasty departure.

Chapter Five: Release

It be here that Sir John recalled to me later in time what happened, for the purpose of my diary.

'We arrived back at Colesdale Hall from a trip to London on a wet stormy morning. I remember the rain which came down in sheets for the last half hour of my journey. With haste my trunk was carried into the hall by Thomas who was my driver. I watched from inside my coach, I had need to check on the condition of the horses, they being still quite young. We both agreed that while Goldie looked fine; Sam looked a little out of sorts. So, as I suggested some remedy for Sam, I noticed Thomas turn his head and call out "Sir, did you hear that cry?"

I stopped and listened. I knew this to be of some importance for well-mannered Thomas to interrupt me.

'No. I . . .'   As I started to speak, I heard a faint wailing sound, followed by a prolonged scream. My heart raced. I looked at Thomas and said 'Over there!' And pointed down the path leading to the rear kitchen of the house. We both charged off with me in the lead. We entered the back yard through the open gate and I remember my disquiet and unease as I remarked, 'Tis a girl's voice, I declare!' Another scream even

louder now rang out. The source of the misery be soon located in the backyard lashed by the driving rain

'Pon my soul what madness!' My unbelieving eyes caught sight of a young girl drenched to the skin, blue with cold who looked near to death. She be laid out flat on the cold stone flags, as she shook this way and that, with a violence rarely seen.

I felt an anger most uncommon in my life and I fear I shouted so. 'Who the Hell would be responsible for this?' I cried. I knew the answer as soon as I began to shout.

'Jenkins, Jenkins come here! . . Oh, my Lord! Come here this instant!' I shouted at the top of my voice.

A worried looking Master Jenkins, ran into the yard.

'Yes, Sir John?'

'Jenkins you're here at last! What in the Lord's name have you done to this poor girl?'

He looked down at Betty with a pale face. If only I had known the true reason for his white face. (His fear at losing his position as butler). Then I believe I would have sacked him on the spot. It be much later that I learned of the true details of his terrible behaviour.

'I'll not have this sort of thing happening here, indeed not,' I told him.

As I organised the moving of Betty into the kitchen, I could see that Thomas was also most annoyed with Master Jenkins, and did wave his fist at him to show himself ready for any trouble.

'You be lucky not to get this,' he said.

Meanwhile Master Jenkins pretended not to notice and said to me, "that he had made an error in her punishment. The weather had surprised him and he was extremely sorry with these most unexpected results."

I remember Sir John apologise to me for my terrible situation.

This did revive me to some small degree, though I felt as if I be a corpse on cold stone, with my heart which beat so strange in my chest. Soaked and frozen, I shivered with a violence that shook my whole body.

*** *

I became aware that they wanted me to move, and I tried to but was unable. And bless Sir John! He had hold of me by one arm with Master Jenkins instructed to hold the other one. Gently they lifted me on to feet that could hardly bear my weight. Then dear Thomas bore the weight of my legs and they carried me.

'I'm so sorry young lady,' I heard Sir John say softly in my ear.

Together the three men carried me through the yard to the

kitchen.

At a later date Miss Grimshaw, who could hear nothing in the kitchen, described to me how she first heard Sir John shout out as Thomas with one hand opened the back door. Then they all charged into the kitchen carrying me in their arms.

Inside this warm haven and unable to stop my tears of relief, I was placed in a chair by the fireside, I had difficulty sitting, due to the shaking of my body. At this point I could not be sure what happened.

All I remember was Sir John's voice as he shouted, "Master Jenkins, get some warm blankets for the poor mite. Lord help us!"

Miss Grimshaw was clearly upset as she later described how I appeared to her at that time. She said I looked in a swoon with my eyes rolling upwards in a terrible way. My face, arms and legs were blue. She described how Sir John looked, so filled with anger, as he cried out, *"She must not sleep, at all costs she must remain awake. This poor girl be near death with cold I declare!"* Then he called out to me in a loud voice, *"Miss Grimshaw, make a pot of tea without delay, and with plenty of sugar."* She said, she took no offence at his tone, as she realised the urgency.

Miss Grimshaw continued her description of me. *'You sat slumped and shook with violence in the chair as Sir John grabbed blankets from Master Jenkins. Thomas realised your plight, and held onto you as you jerked forward off the chair, so much did you move. He managed to lower you gently onto the hearth rug. Sir John had much concern for you it be plain to see. He passed blankets over to Thomas and they both took care to cover you with layers of warm woollen blankets to preserve your modesty. T'was for some time did they take an arm each and rub some warmth back into you.'*

For my part I realised that I must have slipped to the floor. Though where I be, did take me some time to understand because there I lay, stretched out in front of a fire with warm wool blankets wrapped around me. Then I understood and remembered that the fire, was normally kept low to save on coal, and now roared with burning wood to increase the heat. It was at this point that Miss Grimshaw started drying me with warmed towels.

'No, no you don't need to do all this for the likes of me,' I protested weakly in a mumbled voice that I fear barely left my lips.

I tried to protest further and could not talk. I remember I broke down and words I wanted to say wouldn't leave me, I tried to explain to Sir John how I had caused the loss of the game pie for lunch and deserved punishment. But I fear I was not understood. I wept so hard out of relief, as again I tried in vain to talk, to explain myself. Then I realised he be speaking to me.

'Betty...Betty... Stop! You're safe now and I want you to know the loss of the pie be of no consequence and to worry no further.' It's said that Sir John held me around the shoulders as I sat and swayed at this stage. I didn't know what I was doing. They say I collapsed back into my blankets. I have no memories of this.

I tried to thank him but he stopped me again and would have none of it. Bless Sir John! I was in a bad way and only awoke on occasion. Thomas, I realised later, helped to look after me in several ways. I remember being woken up as he did his best to feed me the hot tea. I became aware that both be anxious for me to return to health. And stayed until they be sure that I would recover. I drank sweet tea for the first time and swear it warmed me. That is a memory that has stayed with me.

At some point I woke up and remember his Lordship's voice which could be heard in a nearby room as he spoke in a loud voice about the matter with Master Jenkins. I would say that Sir John be fair mad. For he be the most moderate of people. It pained me to hear his voice raised so, on my account. Then I must have passed out again. I still shivered at this stage. He did tell me at a much later date that Master Jenkins had been warned that any further mistakes would mean he be released from his post of Butler.

Sometime later Sir John, left to get changed out of his clothing which I understand was still wet. Then I woke up in a bed to find that my own wet clothing had been removed and I wore a fresh cotton shift. Miss Grimshaw put my mind to rest by telling me it was Sarah and she who had undressed and dried me. 'Where am I?' I asked.

'We've put you in the spare guest room for now. You are to stay here until you be well.'

I couldn't believe what happened next. Sir John said this to me. 'I trust my dear, that you will quickly recover and see it in your heart to forgive Master Jenkins,' and with that he kissed my hand, the hand of a scullery maid. A true gentleman I declare and my saviour without any doubt.

I be well aware that Sir John and Thomas rescued me from certain death. Though Thomas claims it be all down to Sir John. For this I can't find words good enough to thank them both.

Chapter Six: My Inheritance

This all happened hours ago and although I still felt tired and ill, this time my tears were of relief. Warmed up and well fed, I still shivered occasionally as I lay tucked up in my bed in comfort. I had been instructed to stay there till the morrow. Miss Grimshaw told me to lie-a-bed and promised to visit me with food. I slept for most of the time, tortured by the same dream and most dark in nature. As the hours passed, I found my mind slipping back into the past. Perhaps this be a means of leaving the darkness of my present state behind me.

By this time though I be deep in sleep, I believe I remember this in a correct fashion. My four years spent at Worsthorne Abbey did introduce three sisters there, who became like family to me. Maybe it be fanciful but perhaps in my sleep I did but seek comfort in my extreme situation by remembering my last sight of them as I left Worsthorne Abbey.

First there was Head Sister Nichols, a wonderful person who helped me when I had no one. I did but enjoy my time and I remember her as she taught me to read and write and to make rag dolls. And never to forget our reciting of Shakespeare (a treat for me when she be pleased with my work).

I opened an eye and glimpsed a red sky this told me it be late afternoon. I associated this with the comfort of the Abbey then I realised this was not my old safe place among the sisters. So, I concentrated hard, though not asleep properly, and soon Sister Richards face came to mind she be cross eyed but a beautiful character, she gave me hugs (which be against the strict rules of the Order) when she knew I was missing my mother. I realised that I was concerned about how she be now.

Then I thought of dear sister Bernadette, she had the patience of a saint, I know this because she told me so. She was like that, a wonderful person. A person of great perception. She taught me to be me. My spirit soared into a happy countenance as I thought so of my cherished friends. I tried to keep happy, but there be little of this in my mind as I became awake. So, as 'I lay there, I tried with certain desperation to get back to my refuge in sleep.

It didn't take long. Soon it was back to blackness again as I remembered that day those years ago. Although my mood lifted at the thought of my mother, it be tempered with what followed.

The date was February the year of our Lord 1732.

It was evening and time for our meal. I remember her worried countenance as she admitted that she had no money until she was paid the ninepence owed to her for washing clothes. It hurt my mother to have to beg, but we had no food.

So, it was with poor fortune when she left me on my own for but a short while. In my bright-eyed innocence, I opened the door and allowed Mister Scribbs our landlord to enter our miserable one room cottage. He had come to collect his weekly rent. I remember he seemed nice to me at first. But soon he was hurting me, doing something I didn't understand; I was scared beyond words. I imagined this to be my punishment for my mother not being there to pay him. I couldn't help but scream out in pain. Then it happened; my mother came rushing into the room and dropped to the floor instantly, the single egg she had just been given. I remember her face a mask of fury, as she filled the air with her screams; So loud as to shock Mr Scribbs.

'I'll kill you! You dirty swine, she is only nine years old.'

Her shouts and screams alerted the neighbourhood, so a nearby Constable rushed to the door. Mother now in an uncontrolled frenzy, launched herself at Mr Scribbs, in a manner the likes of I'd never seen before nor since. She screamed continuously, while her nails gouged away at his face. Her arms flailed away like a windmill. He shouted out in pain and could be heard pleading, as he tried desperately to defend himself.

'Tis lucky for you I possess not a carving knife, for you would never do this again.'

There was much trouble and commotion that evening. A bloody, battered Mr Scribbs to his intense displeasure, was led away to the local jail and locked up. I can well believe after being told, and not being there of course, that in no small agreement a crowd followed the Constable and the accused to the jail. Certain shouts of, 'throw away the key! cut his balls off!' and other threats filled the air. These were never to happen, I felt relieved much later to relate, even though I was so cruelly penetrated.

At a later date my mother did see fit to relate to me the true facts of life. I shook with fear at the details.

My mind was filled this night with spectres, and bad dreams of every kind, like clouds they assailed me and drifted to and fro, dark mostly, as a kind of release from my near-death escape.

I turned many times in my bed during last night. The next morn I was still unwell, although thank the Lord I live on. My dream of the past is part of what I be now.

Colesdale Hall, Yorkshire, England.
Early January, the year of the Lord 1737

With the resilience of youth, I soon bounced back to good health after the incident when Jess ate the woodcocks. I found myself smiling at her as I remember that she caught the birds in the first place. I had been told in the past, that with such happy countenance I could never be at a low ebb for long. I thank the Lord (as I had been taught) for my good health and, if truth be known, good luck, although I may have wished for a more fortuitous birth at times. This thought did bring back a distant memory of my mother's wisdom.

I recall how she sat me down and taught me that honesty and to be a good person, were more important than any accident of birth. Memories of this conversation allowed me to suffer not from the melancholy of a conscience. Though being honest I did find could at times bring about complications.

My mother died, bless her, and left me with just four things.

One. A small silver locket with my father's likeness and the name Arthur engraved therein. I knew this to be precious to her, for she asked me to guard it with my life. This I used as a bookmark. The nuns allowed me to use it as such, provided I never wore it. Adornments went against the traditions of the order.

Two. She gave me a quick and loud tongue; may God rest her soul! If I be wrong then I take anything owed to me, as when for selfish reason I allowed the Sir's birds to be taken by the dog. But if I be falsely accused, done harm or mischief to by anyone, then my tongue could have a life of its own. In the extreme, I swear I could lose my mind. I knew not what words would come next from my lips and I be sure this could cause my downfall. 'So, help me God!' How the nuns made me repent for this great sin in the past.

On the other hand, I admit the sin of a smile in contradiction, usually when a nun, would state my repentance for this great sin had not worked. I smile again to myself, though perhaps I mock God. For why can he not command of me a quieter repose? A question to which I always believed there was to be no answer.

Three. An education, at the age of nine years, my mother did her best when she took me to be raised by nuns at Worsthorne Abbey. There they found me to be a quick learner so they taught me to read and write; this eventually placed me in good circumstance for which I am eternally grateful for; and a fine compensation for my forced repentance, for the crime of being a bastard. Oh! Those hours spent on my knees. I felt at the time that the Lord could have forgiven me for my birth right. I after all had no hand in the matter.

Four. My diary. Proud am I to own this, with my mother's mark inside the cover, put there when she gave it to me, to be cherished above all things. She would rest in peace if she could only but know that when I left the nuns, I be blessed with the good fortune to find employment in the kitchen of Sir John Peregrine Morton, late of Jamaica, from the well-known family of sugar exporters/importers J. P. Morton and Company.

Chapter Seven: A Conflict in the House

25th November the year of our Lord 1737

One morn when ahead of my work I took a break between chores, sat in the pantry and away from nosey eyes. I did feel able to rest for so short a time. Between a gap in the pantry door, I chanced a look and caught Miss Grimshaw's eye. I knew she had seen me which worried me not. Her head lowered, she faced me as she worked on the kitchen table. She stopped stirring a cake mixture in her mixing bowl, and put the large wooden spoon down, then it be when she gripped the table edge with both hands and leaned forward; I guessed she may have something on her mind. Then I heard the voice, aimed at me like a musket. 'You, young people soon become spoiled and that would never do for a person of your breeding.'

Now I did start to wonder, could this be some small change in my duties? I didn't have long to wait before I truly understood her words. By this time, I had entered the kitchen and stood facing her by the large dining table. She looked about the kitchen, turned and squinted against the weak November sun as it streamed through the window, with her flat hand shadowing her eyes as she spied across the yard to make sure we were on our own. I had no time to wonder as she quickly spooned some mutton broth into a small bowl and she pushed it down the table in my direction. I wasted no time and soon readied myself to devour the broth, so hungry did I feel and totally unable to forget my manners.

I took time to express my thanks. 'Thank you, Miss Grimshaw,' I said. 'This can only do me a power of good.'

'Now Bet, don't let anyone see this. Especially Master Jenkins.' Her eyes followed a similar curve to the sun as it travelled over the sky.

I nodded. On this occasion I noticed a slight change in the way Miss Grimshaw seemed to have regard of me. Today my hunger would lose its edge, even though the evening food I knew would not change, and the morrow will still bring such hunger. If you had ever been so unfortunate as myself, to be near starved, then you would truly understand what this food meant to me.

Finally, I wasted no time as I ate with barely a pause. Later that morn, I paid with pains to the belly due to the rich nature of this fare, and my lack of regard for good digestion. It was so full of tasty dripping I'm sure I would fore-go the consequences I be about to experience again, for another bowl.

Just seconds after Miss Grimshaw took back my now empty bowl, the inside door banged open with much force as Master Jenkins burst through into the kitchen, as welcome as a winter storm. He stood there and spluttered like an ill lit fire. His face smouldered, like red coals a burning.

Miss Grimshaw to her credit ignored him and started to stir her spoon again. This she accompanied with recollections of her youth. 'Though you may believe you have it hard here; in my day you had to work without a break for twelve hours a day,' Miss Grimshaw carried on as if nothing had happened. 'This was a time when scullery maids worked for food and board only.'

As regards Master Jenkins, this only threw fat upon the fire. I glanced towards him and I didn't like what I could see.

Despite this, the Devil inside me took hold, for I found myself unable not to enquire, 'So you got food in those days?' Oh, that tongue of mine.

I knew what was in her thoughts, which must find her a little unsettled, and with little peace of mind. I was that young person of new blood, one day to replace her.

She continued her reminisce, as if something she needed to say, 'Uhm! Yes, but only barley gruel twice a day an' the odd bruised apple from the Master's trees. That was all we 'ad."

I didn't disbelieve her, because times like that were easy to imagine.

'And all *you* would have, if I had my way,' Master Jenkins' voice was loud as he glared at me from under those bush-like black eyebrows which met in the middle.

'Oh, I don't doubt you one moment!' I threw this straight back at him with no hesitation.

In some curious way I enjoyed the first stirrings of fear in my stomach as he continued to glare. Today, I took my chances with my tongue.

'Miss Grimshaw, I've noted what you have done and you crossed me. I warned you.' Master Jenkins looked dangerous.

'Oh, Master Jenkins, for the love of the Saviour! What harm can a little broth do?'

I noticed she bit her top lip.

At around this time, and when we chanced to be alone Miss Grimshaw would call me Bet, and before I knew it, almost everyone called me by that name; a little thing that showed I had been accepted with God's grace into this working family. That was by everyone except Master Jenkins who continued to call me Betty.

By his standards it might be generally supposed that he treated me in a neutral fashion. He actually held me in no regard for my small efforts and abilities. I had by the whiles of the female gender started to gain an understanding of this truly obnoxious *man*. So, as I grew older, I fully realised that I must be extremely careful in my dealings with him. For who would rescue me if the events of February 1732 were repeated? He was not a man to be trusted.

Chapter Eight: The Joys of Christmas

December, the year of our Lord 1737

Soon the season of goodwill came upon us. Christmas at Colesdale Hall consisted of a well-cooked turkey dinner eaten in the kitchen without ceremony. I took the opportunity to gather a basket full of large sprigs of holly with beautiful red berries (which I so love, and grew in profusion nearby as a small tree) these I spread about the kitchen. Two were affixed to the large looking glass in the family room upstairs. I considered that to be enough, and did so wonder why Sir John be neutral in his celebration for Christmas.

I heard whispers later that Master Jenkins had taken charge of the Christmas brandy bottle. So, this never appeared. Nor, I hasten to add, would any be offered to me. Used as I was to Christmas being celebrated in the Abbey with glorious ceremony, my first Christmas at Colesdale I found to be a bleak celebration by comparison. A service at the local parish church did feel a little like the joyous season with the hymns we sang, although the sermon was far too long and tedious in the extreme. We sat in that seasonally decorated church for hours, it be so cold I lost all feeling in my feet. I did so appreciate (as did we all) that lovely spiced hot cider we enjoyed upon return to Colesdale Hall. Miss Grimshaw had the foresight to prepare this treat beforehand. I did notice she tipped a small glass of brown liquid into her own glass. That's just to cool it down I don't like it too hot. She winked at me. I had finger tasted a drop from the bottom of Sir John's glass in the past, and it made me wrinkle my nose in disgust.

We were but one week into the New Year, and it was mid-morning as I cleaned some pots and pans in the kitchen, I heard a knock to our back door.

'I'll get it,' Miss Grimshaw used a folded cloth to close the door on two treacle tarts, of the new cast iron surround oven. And opened the back door.

'Hello Liz, and a Happy New Year to you.' They hugged briefly.

'You look well Fanny,' she stood back, 'Most healthy, I do declare.'

I watched as Liz sat at the table while Miss Grimshaw made the tea.

'Liz, you called at a most opportune time.'

'Oh really!'

I could see the nosiness ooze out of Liz as she waited for a nice juicy snippet of gossip to excite her fancies. Meanwhile Miss Grimshaw busied herself as she laid out the china on a small hastily spread tablecloth.

Meanwhile Liz, could hardly keep still as she waited, while Miss Grimshaw poured the milk into the cups, shortly followed by the tea. Eventually they both had stirred in sugar.

Liz could not restrain herself any longer, 'Well . . .?' she looked at Miss Grimshaw, who had been distracted and looked slightly surprised for a moment.

'Oh, it's our new fire range, Do, sniff please.' she sniffed in the cooking smells as if to demonstrate how.

'What?'

'I have two treacle tarts cooking and they will be ready soon. I know how you like your tarts.'

'Really, I thought you had some news for me,' her disappointment was palpable.

I could hear Miss Grimshaw talk to her friend Liz Miller, who had become a regular visitor and a rich source of village gossip. This was of some small embarrassment to me, for it was not (and has never been) my habit to listen in to conversations. But I confess I couldn't help hearing the discourse and I wouldn't have found this out otherwise.

'This be the third Christmas,' she said 'that Sir John has spent here in the family home and it has turned out to be no better than the first two. Although I can understand the first one, for we had just got the manor organised and running after all the years of running with a skeleton staff. But there has been no improvement for us since then'

'I remember Christmas last year. It was better this year surely?' said Liz. Her fair eyebrows threatened to reach her hairline so far did they travel.

'Now there, that's enough. I cannot say a word against Sir John; he be otherwise a fine Master to us.'

So definite seemed her opinion that I noticed her double chin wobble as her head shook.

It seemed obvious to me that Liz with her pointed nose would wheedle it out of Miss Grimshaw, like a crow stealing a fisherman's worms.

'Come on now. . . tell me, you must!'

Liz looked about ready to take out a pair of thumb screws, to extract the terrible details, so eager was she for information. (These I had seen at a fair where criminals had terrible justice administered to them at the stocks on the village green).

'Swear you will tell no one!'

There couldn't be any trust in Liz to keep her mouth shut. But Miss Grimshaw continued anyway. Unable to stop herself, for both were out of the same mould. Prattlers they both be.

'Yes, just a piece of Christmas Pudding,' she said 'and a small brandy with a Merry Christmas from Sir John and that was it. Better than nothing I suppose. We had orders that the celebrations were to take place only at the parish church, so to this effect we were allowed to finish our chores early to attend the long special service there. It was not a gay Christmas at all.'

'Really! What, no party for the household staff in the kitchen as would be proper?' asked Liz.

'No! I tell you, Sir John spent most of his Christmas alone at the church in prayer. A most lonely and cold pursuit at this time of the year.'

'Yes, Christmas is a bad time if you are a widower. You know he will make a fine catch for some lady in his class,' observed Liz with a twinkle in her eye.

By now I couldn't keep my mouth shut even if the Lord himself commanded it of me. I wanted the truth known, to the benefit of Sir John.

'Miss Grimshaw,' I said. 'I expect with all the cooking in the kitchen, that it may have slipped your mind about our Christmas day, dinner.'

As soon as these words left my mouth. Liz's head swivelled to see Miss Grimshaw's reaction.

'I, I, I. . . Yes, I am about to tell you, we did have a nice meal thanks to me. But Sir John never came down to see us.'

Again, I discarded all caution. 'Did we find out about that Christmas brandy bottle?' I had a feeling that she had something to do with its disappearance.

'Oh. . .Master Jenkins, he took charge of all that. . .Like

always!'

What happened next, spoiled the day for us all as I remember. Master Jenkins burst into the kitchen in a foul mood and clearly not pleased with what Miss Grimshaw had said.

'You prattle again I see!' he said. 'Should you not be preparing the evening meal, instead of wasting, the Sir's time like this?'

'Really!' retorted an indignant Miss Grimshaw. 'This is just a friendly talk between two friends! How can you say this to me? When have I ever been late preparing a meal, I ask you?'

'Do not cross me woman, I warned you before!' his voice was most unpleasant.

By now both of them had red faces and stood defiant. Liz Miller said a hasty goodbye to her friend. I remember the long dark look she gave Master Jenkins as she made her way out of the kitchen.

Later Miss Grimshaw told me. 'It be better to keep out of his way in the afternoon. If you know what I mean.' She looked me in the eye to make the meaning clear. I didn't understand what she meant at the time and it was some while before I did.

Since the incident with the dog, Master Jenkins had at least been almost civil with me, though not friendly. This I found out later to be due to the "The Warning," Sir John had given him. It was always my intention to have pleasant discourse with all whom I worked with. But from the start I had unpleasant feelings about Master Jenkins, a *man* I knew would one day be the cause of further trouble.

After my experience with the nuns, most work in the kitchen was normal work for me. Because it was my job to clean and fire-black the cooking irons, I always tried to make sure they looked the best I could and I found that a little goose fat on a rag when rubbed well and hard into the freshly blacked irons gave them a special lasting shine. Miss Grimshaw was the first to notice and spoke up to me.

'Bet, I like the shine you leave on the fire-irons.' Just a few words I know, but I liked her beaming countenance. It was just those eighteen hours I spend on my feet, so tired did I feel at the end of the day. But at least I be now paid twenty-five shillings every year as well as my keep.

Chapter Nine: Sir John Speaks to Me

This was a quiet period of the cold winter months. So, one morning as I went to light the fires in the upstairs rooms, I did as always, I started with the main living room, or the family room as we called it. A room so magnificent and full of wonderful paintings I would often stop to admire, (when on my own of course). I was led (for some reason) to believe that Sir John's family were all deceased and only lived on, in the paintings that covered the walls up to the ceiling. It was into the room I must have drifted like a cloud. It be no later than five of the clock, and my want would to have been to be safely curled up in bed. So, it be with some care, I held the coal scuttle. I'm sure that it was tiredness which followed me from my bed, and enclosed me like a cloud only to disperse when I be fully awake.

As I entered the room, I surprised Sir John and to be honest myself as well. Before a portrait on the wall, he stood with a burning candle in a holder, silent as if in prayer. It was too late to back away for I knew he would see me, so I looked at him with great disadvantage, and almost without thinking asked. 'Who is the beautiful lady, Sir John?'

The sight of Sir John, as he jumped with fright, caused me to say. 'I be sorry to startle you, Sir John.' I instantly regretted my hasty tongue, for indeed no right had I to converse with him. A cramp gripped my stomach. And I did shudder so, to my disadvantage which Sir John couldn't fail to notice.

He cleared his throat, and took a good look at my miserable self. 'That's alright,' he said, 'I'm looking at Marie, my perfect wife, whom God saw fit to take from me these few years past, and being the reason for my return to England.'

'You must have loved her.' I said, while I felt an urge to run from this situation. I truly disliked this unsettled feeling.

'Indeed, I did and still do, I sometimes wish The Lord had taken us together,' he said as he stared intently at the painting. Then he remembered himself and said, 'You speak like someone past your years.'

'Sorry, Sir John.' I tried to bite my lip. This could be the cause of no end of trouble for me now.

'No, no, that's alright, but I would like you to keep this between you and me.'

'Sir, I will do nothing else, I'm not one to prattle.'

He nodded, gave me a long look and said, 'It's best you get on with your chores eh?'

I almost fled, so curiously upset did my belly feel.

Twas, but a short while later, I found him again early in the morn, in the same family room, where he sat partly hidden and

I be the one to be caught by surprise.

'I be so sorry Sir John; I didn't see you sat there!' I blurted out in no small anguish.

Again, that feeling hit me, so with no invitation, I followed instructions given previously by Master Jenkins, and moved slowly backwards towards the door.

'No! No! Come on, Betty. I'm inviting you,' he said, as he waved his hand twice towards himself.

He looked relaxed in an arm chair and sported an expensive plain dark blue silk dressing gown with gold edging and with his gold rimmed spectacles in his right hand, I could see I had interrupted his reading. 'Another evening of little sleep,' he said.

I had feelings of unease, as if a Sir needed to excuse himself to such as the likes of me. Next to him on a small reading table, a burning candle casts its light over a large open book, I spotted a green leather book mark between the pages.

Books be my one love in life. I have the Sisters at Worsthorne Abbey to thank for that, though only a diary do I own. I took my fear in check, and the liberty to glance down, as no right did I possess. My beating heart danced as I recognised the words. This be one of those times when my tongue spoke with the truth of my soul. So, I allowed those words from my heart to bury any fear I might possess.

'Sir! I see you read Shakespeare,' I ventured with care. I wrung my hands at the same time, for I knew that one day my tongue would get me into the trouble so long promised me, by certain people who knew me well. I decided to remain quiet. Who would guess what turmoil I felt in my chest as my heart continued to race so.

'My, my. . . you can read. . . my little maid can actually read!'

He sounded so tickled at the thought. He looked at me thoughtfully and in a most kindly way. Silent now, he clearly noticed my worried, perhaps frightened countenance. He had, I'm sure, seen the turmoil I so wanted to hide.

I know not where I gained the confidence. After a deep breath, I started to recite from memory in a voice which I believe gained volume as I progressed.

'Sir. . .

When forty winters shall besiege thy brow,

And dig deep trenches in thy beauty's field,

Thy youth's proud livery, so gazed on now,

Will be a tattered weed of small worth held.'

'One of my favourite sonnets,' I said quietly after a pause. Oh, I've said too much! I thought, wringing my hands again. I've been far too familiar. No right had I to talk in such a way. 'Sir, I must do my work I'm sorry I have no right.' I started to say.

'No! I'm somewhat lost for words, please sit down,' he said.

After a short pause he gathered his thoughts, and gestured to me in a most gentle way to sit on the armchair opposite to him.

So, I sat on the edge of the chair in no great comfort and not a little embarrassed, I suppose I had colour to my young cheeks. My nagging fear only added to my discomfort.

'This could be a most fitting sonnet for me. With some nine years to go, then I too will have seen forty winters, an age we don't look forward to. You are full of surprises, aren't you?'

He looked lost in thought. 'So, Betty, how come you are a scullery maid?' he enquired. 'With a brain like yours, this is a terrible waste, I know several educated people who cannot recite Shakespeare,' After a pause he added. 'Please do tell me more about yourself.'

Though I shook with fear, in but little time I outlined my life story, about my mother and how the nuns taught me a love for reading and writing. These were the main points of a story with little else to tell. I ended by saying to Sir John. 'It be my good fortune to be employed in this household. This I do declare to be true. My mother brought me up to never tell a lie and I never will. Of lowly station I be, but you will see I serve you most truly.'

As I spoke, Sir John looked at me clearly with a new interest, and I am sure I detected a little moisture build up in his eyes.

'Well read, and well-spoken too, I do declare,' he said, and as he spoke, he nodded slowly, as if to confirm something. 'I'm delighted to have you here in my house, and I do believe you like it here.'

'Yes Sir, you are very kind,'

He silenced me with a shake of his hand and asked, 'And how old are you, Betty?'

I noticed he had used my first name in a friendly way. It was my turn now to be short of words. All I could say was. 'Sir, I be fourteen years.'

'From now on I shall call you Bet, is that alright?'

I could do no more than nod. Sir John asked me this, a kitchen scullery maid? Could this be true? I asked myself.

'Tis sometime in the future that he called me 'My dear Bet,' I will explain later when propriety demands.

My life continued in the fashion that be proper for someone in my station. I worked hard all day and never had much more than the clothes on my back, I required not much at this stage of my life.

It was before my second Christmas that Sir John in another of the early meetings that happened from time to time. He made a remark that I looked unwell, and asked me if I ate enough.

How could I answer that? All I said was.

'Sir John, it is my good fortune to be in your employ.'

The kind Sir seemed concerned as he looked at me for a few moments. . . lost in thought, he shook his head and said, 'You are but skin and bones.'

If he knew I fed occasionally off the leavings from the table, I be sure he would have been appalled. What could I do, this was not my place to say anything and why would I want to trouble Sir John?

Chapter Ten: Changes

Nothing further was said to me after my short conversation with Sir John. During the day, as I completed my countless tasks, I forgot about his question regarding my food and my starving countenance.

It was indeed to my surprise, when the time for the evening meal arrived and Master Jenkins, with a certain unpleasant look upon his face, invited me to the table. He told me that I had in future to join them to share their repast. All this was said while he looked over my head.

At first, I felt a little uncomfortable at the table with five others; Master Jenkins, Miss Grimshaw, Thomas, the coach man with whom I enjoy a chat on the occasion, Sally the chamber maid, whom I of course know well, and Henry Trimble the gardener, whom I had spoken to only twice.

I was given no cause to worry, because most of them made me most welcome. So different was this to eating in the pantry, left on my own to eat a crust of bread and a little cheese.

After grace and before we had chance to eat, Miss Grimshaw spoke to me.

'You certainly have made an impression on Sir John. He has given instructions that you are to eat the same food as us. I mean, *'REALLY,"* She hesitated for a second and continued to place large chunks of bread by each of the bowls.

'We need to keep an eye on you, that be a certain fact if any could be.'

I ignored Master Jenkin's nasty comment to me.

With a fold of cloth, Miss Grimshaw lifted off the steaming lid from the large earthenware pot, situated on a board in the middle of the oak kitchen table. The savoury smells from the rabbit stew escaped and flooded across the table. As I breathed them in, I felt a conflict deep inside my inner being. A part of me felt nourished by the depth of flavours which flooded my senses, while part of me longed to eat what must be the most wholesome of food.

All these unworthy notions I kept well hidden, and quietly I starved as I waited. My eyes never left that large wooden ladle, as she served everyone at the table. She gave me a long look as she filled up my large bowl and I noticed she most correctly served me last. This food I had so often coveted, steamed away in a pot bowl before me. Hardly could I believe it. Miss Grimshaw talked away without stop. 'I pointed out to Sir John that Betty was merely a scullery maid. Do you know what else he said to me? May the Lord strike me dead and send me to Hell if I lie!'

'I have no idea,' sighed Master Jenkins.

Her attention returned to Master Jenkins as she continued to speak. 'He said, "that will have to change". . . Can you believe it? "*CHANGE!*" What on earth does *that* mean?'

Unable to stop myself, I spooned this manna from heaven into my mouth, being careful about my table manners as taught by the nuns. My enjoyment and gratitude be there for all to see.

'Did he now. . . well, well, how can it change?' asked Master Jenkins.

Twas then I heard the word. It was enough to send me into a swoon. My hand stopped with the spoon halfway to my waiting lips, and I stared at the candle as it spat and flared. The word *CHANGE* seared its way into my mind.

I did so wonder what Sir John meant by a change, for tis true changes can be for the better, but not for a scullery maid, surely? Could this be trouble brewing for me some time in the future?

Am I correct not to worry about Miss Grimshaw? I'm sure she had a heart of gold really. I also believed with the help of God that I worked as well as be possible for me.

Master Jenkins told me he held no ill against me, a little while after my mistake with the wild birds. Though I did but wonder, for his face and countenance belied his words, casting distasteful looks in my direction as if he disliked me. These I had ignored because of my lowly status and I being by far the youngest. So, with God's help I said nothing and held my tongue.

I was worried about what could be on Sir John's mind and what he might have in store for me. Was he happy with my work I wondered? My worst fear would be to end up starving and washing people's clothes for a living like my mother had done.

Chapter Eleven: Piece of Mind

March the year of the Lord 1738

I dare say I worry. Tis no fine thing to have this weight upon my young shoulders. Working to the instructions of Master Jenkins for many hours a day occupies my mind and does give me some rest from that worry. At night time my mind imagines some terrible spectre haunting me. A '*change*'. Is this to be my undoing? An uncertainty hangs over me. I do wonder if I doubt my good fortune because I'm alone and a bastard in this world.

Days drag by with no hurry. This was no medicine for my hidden melancholy, as it slowly ate me away inside. It could never be seen in my countenance to show anything but pleasure, so my suffering was my secret, and be fit only for someone of my circumstance.

On this fine but windy morn I walked into the orchard and selected sweet apples from the two sweet Henry trees in our orchard for Sir John's table. These be not the biggest of trees but bear the sweetest of apples. I worked quickly with a sharp kitchen knife, while my mind was all but taken over by that other matter. I knelt down to gather up some fresh wind-blown apples for the pie Miss Grimshaw was about to make and with but little awareness, I indulged in the sin of daydreaming.

It happened by chance that Sir John passed nearby at this moment on his way to the stables. Unaware of my great mistake, I stared down into the half full basket before me. Did he see a sad expression upon my face? I did but wonder afterwards and heard not his approach on the grass. I be not proud of this.

'Is everything alright?'

Sir John, spoke in a friendly tone. This, as much as anything, shocked me from my daydream. He had caught me as I knelt there wasting time. So naturally my tongue took charge in its usual way and I did blurt out with no manner of thought, 'Kind Sir, what is to become of my worthless self? I do worry so!'

Despite his kindly expression, I felt that churning of fear in my belly as he walked up to me. He gazed down at my face and in little more than a whisper, did say these words. 'Bet, you have no cause to worry, I'm pleased with your work.'

Nevertheless, I suspect my concern still lingered like a winter's cold. So, my tongue took charge, 'It be my worst fear to return to my near homeless position again. Good Sir, I do worry so about changes.'

I said this with deliberate intention. I felt that nothing was there to lose. A few tears ran down my cheeks as I hung my head.

After a quick look around, he said, 'Bet! Bet, look at me.'

I looked up, but my shyness forbade me to venture a direct look into his eyes. He glanced about again and, in a low voice, said 'That's better... do not...worry. I can say no more for now.'

The words crept into my mind with purpose and I felt a small smile of re-assurance appear upon my face, almost as if a cloud had parted and the sun now shone. His intelligent eyes swept my face as he gazed intently at me for a few moments. I chanced a quick glance and met with those bright brown eyes of his and, mesmerised, I paused, while for some unknown reason my heart started to beat wildly in my chest.

This was spoiled immediately as I froze, locked by a freezing terror that now gripped my heart. The crunch of his riding boots on the gravel path awoke me as if from a swoon. I did but glimpse the tail of his check-patterned riding cloak which flapped in the breeze as he charged off through the open metal gate and into the stables. I knelt there as the seconds passed. My heart did continue to beat so; this be when I noticed that never before had the wild mint which grew in clumps between the trees smelled so sweet and pure.

I shook my head. What was I thinking? I must make quick time back to the kitchen, unable to work out why I was so fearful, after Sir John's reassurance. As I regained my feet, my cotton pinafore danced in the light breeze. I turned to check behind me, so nervous was I.

Over in the stable yard Sir John placed his foot in the stirrup of Goldie and mounted her, while Thomas held steady with the reins. Sir John had an appointment to attend so he galloped out of the yard, and turned down the tree -covered lane.

I had one thing I wanted to do before returning to the kitchen so I left the half full basket of apples by the gate.

'Hi Thomas,' I called. 'How are you faring? Is your brother settled in his new job over at Stansfield farm.?

I passed the time with him, while I fed Sam an apple. This had been my habit recently. Our short conversation lightened my mood. I stepped back towards the kitchen and with plenty to occupy me, I worked silently without break for some time.

Miss Grimshaw, who noticed my quiet dedication, gave way to her nosey nature and did remark, 'Bet, you're unusually quiet, I do but wonder why.'

I smiled and slowly shook my head.

'There be something on your mind, I'd wager,' she said. She thought for a moment, 'Did Sir John say anything as he passed you by, while you picked apples in the garden?'

Because I be unable to tell a lie, this did put me in a difficult position. I had no desire to make her privy in any way to Sir John's conversations. Nor did I wish to annoy her.

'Nothing of note. We passed the time in but a pleasant way.'

'Oh! Oh, but what did he say? Bet, you simply must tell me!'

At this time, I was approaching my fifteenth year and starting to fill out and I believe I began to look a little like a woman. This also altered my outlook and perhaps, God willing, my confidence in life, although I was still a little uneasy about my future and, if truth be known, my spotty face. So, I remember I gave her a special look to let her know I had no more to say on the subject.

Miss Grimshaw, Bless Her, looked a little like Master Jenkin's dog, Jess, with a bone, (perish the thought), and just couldn't seem to drop the subject.

'I watched you with Sir John. Come on, what did he say to you?'

Her eyes sought mine. This was a battle of wills I just couldn't afford to lose.

'Ask no more questions and I'll tell you no lies.' With this I gave her my look again.

There was much tutting and sighing. With several sentences started...until she realised my lips were closed on the matter.

What I truly liked about Miss Grimshaw was that she had a generous character which matched the size of her body and never seemed to hold a grudge. A while later, she poured me out a rare wine glass of cider which she enjoyed as much as myself. I did reassure her when she calmed down, that nothing said between Sir John and I, had any bearing on herself.

I couldn't stop at first that feeling, a memory of how my heart beat so, of discomfort or worse (was it fear?) Later, I realised that his words offered only comfort, and I should no longer worry. So, I put my trust in the kind Sir John.

Chapter Twelve: A Surprise for Miss Grimshaw

In The Year of Our Lord May 1738

It happened on a busy Saturday morn, as I toiled to clean out the large stew pot, which was of a size, thankfully, as to require this only once a week.

I heard Miss Grimshaw clear her throat, as was her habit before she spoke. I prepared myself to learn that perhaps she had found some more work for me.

'Betty, I've noticed in the past that you seem to enjoy helping with the cooking?'

Her look demanded an answer.

Though unsure, I replied, 'Of course Miss Grimshaw.'

'Sarah has no time for cooking. So, Betty, do you want to help me with the cooking? And you can learn, so one day be able to improve your lowly position here at Colesdale Hall.'

Another question. This was a different day for me. I knew I must say yes. I also knew that my heart said yes, for that be my path to better circumstances. With no more than a few seconds of thought, I gave the only answer I could and wanted to give.

'Er yes, YES, of course, Miss Grimshaw!'

'Sir John indicated that all he wanted for dinner was one of my big special cheese and onion pies he so loves. This makes it easy for me and gives me a little spare time. So, Betty, I'll show you how to make short crust pastry.'

Today, she had seemed a little less severe in her attitude with me, kindly even, as if I had just pleased her, which I always consider to be my duty. If this be so, then maybe she may realise I do the best that my young body can manage. And perchance the Lord may allow her to think the more of me.

'I know how to make it. I've watched you once produce the biggest of pies I have ever seen. Although I confess, I may need a little help with the quantities of flour and fat.'

So, between us we soon had the pastry made and cooling in the larder on the thick sandstone slab next to the milk. While I peeled and sliced the four medium sized onions and two big potatoes, Miss Grimshaw, at my suggestion, sat by the fire to warm her aching feet. The fire soon heated up more than her feet and she succumbed to the tiredness she felt. Her head slowly moved to rest upon her shoulder. As I smiled at her occasional snore, I realised this be my chance to surprise her, and set to work.

So next, I recovered the rested pastry and cut it in two. With one piece I proceeded to roll it out, like I had seen Miss Grimshaw do. I picked a large metal plate and greased it. The rolled pastry I carefully placed on the plate. Then came a layer of the sliced onions. In the pantry I found the huge round block of good local Yorkshire cheese, hidden under a shroud of muslin. Out of which I carved a generous chunk. This I crumbled up and spread over the onions. The thinly sliced potatoes I treated in the same fashion. Over this I sprinkled salt and sneaked a little of the expensive pepper and plenty of butter which I spread about. I rolled out the other half of the pastry and fitted it over to make the top of the pie. I used a beaten egg to help bind the pastry together. I took time to decorate it, painted on the rest of the egg and remembered the small hole on top. All this for Sir John which I did so hope he enjoyed. Despite being as quiet as a ghost, I still managed to make enough sound when I placed the pie in the oven. And at that point Miss Grimshaw woke up.

'Uhh, what?' she asked, and looked stunned when she could see neither the pie nor the mess caused by making it. I had quietly cleared up most of the mess.

'It's fine Miss Grimshaw, you just nodded off for a short time. Master Jenkins has not shown his face, so all's well. And I put the pie we made in the oven. How long does it take to bake? Because it's had but five minutes in the top oven.'

Again, I got that vacant look, and she turned to the oven. Her face was a treat to see as she tried to make sense of what I had just said. She was a minute late in her answer.

'Oh, about another twenty to thirty minutes should do it.'

I worked at wiping down the table and putting things away. On this occasion I could glimpse her as she stared at me. Perhaps she tried to work me out. I swear this not to be difficult as I be clear as glass. I caught her eye and she looked down at the fire.

I worked by the kitchen window and loved the moors which were visible over the yard wall.

This part of Yorkshire be covered in hills and perfect for raising sheep. Once clear of the work, I took the chance to go outdoors for a little fresh air and a walk across to the garden. I so loved the scents of the nearby wood that drifted over our garden. Thomas worked to repair the fence that spanned a missing portion of our wall. So, I spent a minute or two with him. He was always interesting and had a wealth of information regarding horses and outdoor things. Meanwhile I enjoyed the sight of wild flowers like purple heather, yellow gorse and red poppies which bloomed in a colourful display, and the carpet of daisies spread out over the fields, like a painted scene of the countryside. I needed but the slightest of excuses, and breathed deeply to partake of the fresh scented air at this time of the year. All too soon it was time to return to the kitchen. I had picked a small bunch of flowers to be put in a vase.

'Bet, I worry only to a small degree, how you made the pie.'

Miss Grimshaw, I thank you for showing me how to make

short crust pastry.'

'Yes, but how much cheese did you. . .?'

'Same as you, also the onions and the two potatoes thinly sliced, and besides salt I used pepper and butter.'

'I've never in my life used butter in a cheese and onion pie.'

I had cause to smile to myself, so afraid did she sound. Perhaps she expected me to poison Sir Henry?

We had not long to wait for Sir John's opinion.

It was his reaction to my lowly pie that made the biggest change to Miss Grimshaw's attitude towards me.

Sir John spoke to her, as she cleared his small table. Sarah the chambermaid, 'bless her,' witnessed Sir John's reaction to the pie.

She described it like this, 'He said, "I had two portions today, and I declare this be the best pie ever and wish you to always make it so."

She believed her to be filled with surprise; because as she returned to the kitchen, Sarah who had cause to follow could hear her talk to herself as if in shock. Sarah added that had she not heard this with her own ears, then she doubted I would ever have learned of it.

Miss Grimshaw, seemed to take it well enough. Such was her nature. All she said to me about it was that I will make a good cook one day. This I take as more praise than I ever could deserve.

When my general cleaning duties were completed in the kitchen, my further duties included the preparation of fruit and vegetables and other menial tasks such as churning to make the milk into butter. This be one of the few jobs I found boring and took far too much time for so little result.

One day, after she noticed my interest in the proceedings, Miss Grimshaw let me mix a cake. This I did with good results and pleased her no end with the lack of a mess. Later she sniffed the cooling cake and declared with a smile, "Rich and sweet." Her tone made it into a compliment which pleased me greatly.

A meat pie came next and she showed me her secret of how to make that special pastry. I overheard her comment to Master Jenkins about having only to show me once. This did please me so, especially when she later spoke to me as I worked about entrusting me with the mixing of an egg custard.

'Upon my soul, your pie was enjoyed, again. I do declare we have the makings of a fine cook here. You should always remember that you cook with love and put enjoyment into the food for tis true this be the most important ingredient.'

'In truth Miss Grimshaw, I do truly enjoy cooking, and I only wish to be as fine a cook as you, if that ever with the Lord's help be possible.'

'Oh Ho, Ho, Ho! I do but find that funny. You, my dear Bet will not need the Lord's help, that I can see. Though, there be those who even with the Lord's help could never make a good cook. They have not the love you must put into the food, as I have told you.'

I marvelled at what Miss Grimshaw said, though truth be known, her words be 'to no disfavour.' Though not hungry myself, now I receive two meals a day. I did feel slightly ashamed that I should so rarely taste the results of this kitchen. I stopped my wayward thoughts and furiously attacked the custard with the whisk.

'Miss Grimshaw, I do wish I could try the smallest of tastes of our cooking so as to be able to work to better avail.'

'And quite rightly so, for although you be only a scullery maid you try to please and I believe this could be of benefit in learning the skills of cookery.'

She thought for but a moment, 'Some twenty-eight years ago I started as a scullery maid and had it a lot harder than you. And I had a stern house lady who gave me no peace at all during the day. But you don't wish to hear all about me. I be right?' Miss Grimshaw turned her head towards me.

'I know how you feel and please excuse me,' I said scolding myself silently for what I had said before.

'You can stop whisking now or you will ruin that custard.'

She gave me a long look. 'Did you know I had to sleep in a pantry? With not much comfort I tell you,' She rubbed her forehead with the back of her hand and continued.

'Yes, this was called Long Lee Hall, on the outskirts of a small farmers village called Longley. The Hall be a good half days walk from here. On the nearest hill there stands Studley Pike which can be seen for miles across Yorkshire. The house was ancient and so full of drafts. Winter was an ordeal indeed; we always got the snow the worst around that area. If I told you the snow used to drift into the kitchen under the outer door, would you say I jest? We used to joke that a mouse could walk under the doors wearing a top hat. Nothing but bare stone walls and floors in the servant's wing were our lot. You don't know how lucky you are these days!" She shook her head; lost she be in thought as she continued to baste the already beautifully browned chicken.

A few days later I did espy a few strawberries left in the basket after the day's baking had finished.

'Miss Grimshaw, would it be possible for me with your good grace to bake a fair tart using the strawberries left? I have watched you bake several and do believe I can do the same.'

She gave me one of her looks and surprised me when she said, 'This be another of Sir John's favourites. The oven be still hot and I espy some sweet pastry left over in the bowl that

96

needs using up, so yes you can. . . and this I must see!'

I noticed an amused expression on her face.

'You must hurry for Master Jenkins will be here shortly and the less he sees the better.'

Without much effort I remembered all I had seen done, and soon had a tart in the oven cooking. In a brief time, it was cooked and as it cooled in the pantry, I poured liquid jelly over it. She looked at me and said,

'Well, well you have put fresh basil leaves into the tart and poured jelly over it. I don't know what to say, you may well have ruined it, I do declare.' This was accompanied by a shake of her head.

No sooner had I closed the larder door when in walked Master Jenkins.

'That smells nice, what is it?' He asked.

'This is a tart we have made for Sir John,' said Miss Grimshaw guardedly.

'I expect there will be a slice for me.' Master Jenkins stated as he removed his coat and hung it on the back of the door on "his" hook. He pulled up "his" chair that scraped noisily across the stone floor and dropped himself into it with his arms rested upon the table.

'You can expect what you like. If there is any left you can have some, if not. . .' She left the question dancing into the ether.

'No, I said there 'will' be a slice for me. What are you talking about you silly cow, you know as well as I do, that bugger only eats one slice.'

Miss Grimshaw nodded as she looked at me again. In my innocence, I did but wonder what she had in mind. It be some time before I found out.

Chapter Thirteen: I Learn about Miss Emily

In The Year of Our Lord July 2nd 1738.

Sir John, due to the warm weather, only required a fire in the library. As I passed the family room, on my way there, I heard my name softly spoken. I turned to see Sir John arise from his chair. He called me over, and courteously invited me to sit down first, on that red chair; the same one as before, so favoured for our little talks. How stupid be I to love a chair! He sat opposite on his favourite armchair.

'Good morning, Bet! I have arisen early,' he said, stifling a yawn. I noticed a worried look on his face.

'Sir, may I be so bold as to ask, is there something wrong?'

Yet again I wondered if I be too bold or presumptuous.

'It's just that, well tis not for you to worry, nor me to ask you,'

He gave an abstracted stare, lost to this world. He wondered what to say. I waited for him, but nothing happened. I did but cough slightly and look at him. I was most hopeful that I showed him good manners.

'Sir, please tell me,' I asked, and I waited again.

'My sister Emily is coming,' he said nervously, as he cleared his throat.

'Sir is surely pleased to see his sister?' I ventured.

I did wonder how it could be otherwise.

'I haven't seen her in years and she is gracing us with a visit in one week's time.'

I waited for the kind Sir to tell me more about this sister. I had by no means experience of these things.

'She. . .she is my only living relative and yes, I should be pleased to see her again. Let me just say she is still a spinster, despite being seven years my senior.'

He let out a little whimper of despair at the word senior.

Unable was I to fully comprehend his melancholy at what should be a joyous event.

'What can I do, Bet?' he asked as he rested his forehead on his right hand.

I felt sorry for his predicament, and not a little surprised Sir John should confide in me like this. I was prepared to offer my poor but genuine help, such as I could, with the grace of God, perform. Words escaped my lips as be their want.

My mind raced. 'Sir John, if it be your desire, I can prepare the sitting room and a bedroom for her,' I said.

'In what way? She is fussy.' Sir John looked defeated.

'Does she like flowers, and do you have a portrait of her?'

'Yes, I know she likes flowers and, I have a small portrait of her somewhere, still packed from the move,' he said with a thoughtful, and slightly guilty look.

With no clear plan in my head, I said with a confidence I had no business to feel, 'If Sir, will kindly allow me, I can give the rooms some cheer with flowers from the garden. I am sure she will notice the effort taken to welcome her, especially if we can find that portrait of her.'

Sometimes, I felt strangely at ease with Sir John, and I did feel that he liked me. But I would have to watch my wayward tongue and I must remember my place; I was only a kitchen wench.

'Of course, Bet, I will give you time to prepare, the day before her arrival. I think it is an excellent idea. I see in the hall there is a magnificent display of flowers. Did you arrange them?'

My cheeks started to colour with this unexpected praise from Sir John. For once I be lost for words and hesitated just a second.

'Well, I pick them every day in my dinner break and I like arranging them, 'Tis just some silly pastime, for a poor girl, such as I.'

Oh dear! My cheeks did begin to burn now. Sir John noticed my discomfort and looked closely at me.

After a slight pause, he said. 'I want you to continue in your way, and as for calling such things silly, well, that is stuff and nonsense. I think it brightens up a dull hall and I love the scents from the flowers.'

As he glanced at me, I be sure I can see a small twinge of embarrassment creep across his features. Methinks, he felt he had opened up a little too much for the circumstances.

With that I took my leave.

Preparations for the arrival of Miss Emily continued for days, as the entire house, (that is) every crook and cranny (and there are quite a few in this huge mansion) was cleaned. Bushes were trimmed, the lawn at the front, cut, tidied up and new shrubs were planted. I swear I had never seen Sir John in such a state as he hurried back and forth, checking this and that. A fair number of large pots containing shrubs were obtained and, with the help of Thomas and Peter, placed to the directions of Sir John who fussed about with a measuring stick, so precise did he feel they must be. I did so wonder about his sister Emily. Who was she that made Sir John worry so?

All the staff were fitted and received new uniforms. Most pleased was I because a woman I be now with the attractions of my sex. This required a larger uniform and was a necessity for me at this time. I had been told by Thomas Green, the coachman, "You have a nice small pair of duckies." Though I'm neutral in my discourse with this gentleman, it pleased and amused me, I be ashamed to say.

True to his word, Sir John changed my duties the day before

Miss Emily was due to arrive. All that afternoon was spent with the kind help of old Henry Trimble, the gardener, as we roamed the area well past our garden and into nearby Hurst wood. We picked flowers of all types and fresh ferns from the nearby stream. These flower displays did make me well-nigh swoon, so strong were the scents. I enjoyed my best day yet, as I arranged various displays, to the benefit of the Sir's various rooms. These flowers required several large vases. I took special and obvious care with the display that framed the small painting of a youthful Emily. I managed to form a border of bright green ferns. To this I arranged a number of blue forget-me-nots, some buttercups, and red poppies. The result was eye catching. The reaction of Sir John be well worth recording. 'Oh Bet' he declared, 'this be better than I could ever imagine. I had no idea flowers could be arranged with such beauty. Miss Emily will be so pleased, I be sure.'

Chapter Fourteen: The Arrival of Miss Emily

Afore Sir John first told me about his sister, I thought none of God's creatures could be more severe than one or two of the nuns, who had taken care of me. Being the sister to Sir John, you would be at pains to believe that Emily and he be related.

On a windy July day, Sir John's coach pulled up on time in front of the main door. 'T'were Thomas drove our coach back from York, after he picked up Emily who had arrived on the two pm stagecoach from London.

Oh, what a fuss were made, as we were all ushered outside in our new uniforms to await in no great comfort but good display. Sir John, waited in a quiet corner where I espied him, wringing his hands as if in despair, (a kind man who deserved none of this) while he waited with a most anxious disposition. His descent from his room at the top of the stairs had been undertaken with great haste.

I was told afterwards that he left his telescope up there on the outside terrace, whatever devil's device that be. I watched him walk the few yards to the coach, tall and handsome beneath his sombre dark blue cloak.

Master Jenkins, wearing his best clothes, opened the coach door. Without ceremony, Miss Emily, revealed herself before the household, well dressed and resplendent in red patterned damask coat and satin bodice. Her figure was topped with a black velvet bonnet adorned with the largest of brown feathers, a fleeting apparition of a tyrant queen, such a lady to be rarely seen. She took Sir John's hand, and descended the three steps. I noticed that pleasantries were exchanged between them.

This tall lady marched towards this house of no mean size, and as she did so, she cast her eyes about as if inspecting some inferior inn. Sir John gave up on small talk and was at pains to keep up with her. Meanwhile servants were rushed at her command, going hither and thither with her voluminous luggage.

A smile appeared upon my face that I couldn't conceal. I knew full well it not be my place to show opinion. I stood at the back with Miss Grimshaw, who was well informed as to Miss Emily's habits.

'Sir John warned me that she be of delicate stomach and to be careful about her food. But I failed completely to extract any recipe or information about his sister. I doubt if he knew much himself. He had not seen her in years.

'I think perchance, it may be wise to keep some distance away if possible.'

Miss Grimshaw turned to look, realised my joke, and smiled along with me.

All went well for me until, the next day, when Miss Emily did summon me. Again, my countenance let me down and I broke into a smile as I greeted her with a curtsey. I looked at her and my attention was drawn to a large black mole on her left cheek. Her response was gruff.

'Are you responsible for these blue flowers?' she asked, as she gave me a look that I do accept as befitting my lowly birth right. Before I had a chance to reply, she continued. 'I do prefer red roses.' She thought for a second and added, 'when they're in season of course, but these will do for now, fresh every day of course,' she barked and I received another stern look. 'And not so much greenery with the display, I like colour.'

She paused and spoke. 'So, you are Betty May our scullery maid who can read and write. My oh my! Is this a waste of education, I wonder?' Miss Emily, looked at me closely, before she dismissed me with a regal wave, and picked up the kerchief she had been embroidering.

'Mam,' I said with a curtsey. This was the only word I spoke during this first meeting.

I believe that I can judge people. I admit I do see the good in them. For my pains, all I can see in Miss Emily is a lonely old lady – yes, lady! I 'm convinced beneath that hard, gruff and I believe, lonely exterior, somewhere there lurks an interesting, even likeable person,

It be my good fortune that Master Jenkins has the onerous task of serving at the table of Sir John and Miss Emily, and not I. On the second day of her stay, I spy Master Jenkins sat in distress at the kitchen table after dinner service.

'My dear Lord help me, she sent me down to the kitchen not once to warm the gravy . . . but twice…' he moaned.

'Her beef was not carved to her liking and I had to carve four more pieces. Do you know what? She picked the original piece to eat. Then she fancied a fresh sugared plum. I ask you! I told her plums were not ripe yet. Do you know, she crossed me? She said, "Of course they are ready to be picked." And that she had seen them on the way to Colesdale Hall. Twelve more days of this and I swear I shall lose my sanity.' This was followed by another soft moan.

Indeed, a sight to see, this large, strong man sat with his head in his hands. To be true I laugh not at others' distress, although this I am ashamed to say made me smile. I tried to hold my tongue.

We took it in turns to answer that servant's bell that rung without ceasing. It was with some difficulty I found time to change the flowers every day though, if truth be known, I rearranged them as much as I be able.

Then it happened. One evening just after dinner, what an uproar! Madam Emily could be heard to shout out and near scream: 'I declare Sir John has lost a diamond cufflink!'

13th July the year of our Lord 1738

Tis no exaggeration to state that from down below in the kitchen; we could all hear the commotion above us. At the time certain vegetables were being prepared, to be cooked with peas and beef for the morrow's servant's meal. Dirty dishes stood piled up in rows on the table, I was about to start to wash these items as we paused to listen. Then sure enough.

Ring, ring, ring, ring, the servant's bell rang several times with an applied vigour, which conveyed an immediate attention, an urgency in fact.

Then we heard the shrill voice of Miss Emily call down to us from upstairs, 'Everyone, upstairs. . . now, if you please.'

Her footsteps could be heard as she charged across the floor above us; I knew this to be no ordinary request and I did naturally bestir myself as did the others.

Master Jenkins sensed trouble and pointed upwards to the ceiling in a fruitless gesture, then thought better and ushered us all towards the stairs. So, we made our way from the kitchen and up the stairs to the dining room at no small pace, Miss Emily's raised voice floated down the passage, and could be heard long before we got there.

'John, you must be more careful with things of this value; especially when you are around the staff. This is most forgetful of you. Have you no idea where you mislaid it?'

Sir John looked thoroughly browbeaten when I espied him. He seemed to be looking for a means of escape as we entered the dining room. She had berated him for being absent-minded, and I had to agree. I also agreed with reference to the staff. We had one among us that would not return the cufflink if he found it, of that I be certain, and I be sure others would think so too.

Miss Emily stopped short as we entered the room, as was to be expected.

Sir John ushered us to join in the search which continued for some time, as we hunted in every room of the entire floor. Not a sign of Sir John's Diamond Cufflink could be found under settee, chair, rug, table, or even Miss Emily's sewing box. At this, she waved us back to our work. We left the room and turned down the passage and headed for the servant's stairs. It be then I heard her say in the distance.

'Well John, it must be somewhere and the servants have not found it, I know, because I've been watching them closely.'

I liked what I heard, even though she must have watched me too. I think this to be only correct. I had noticed her eyes seemed bright, and alert, behind her neutral, seemingly *sour* countenance and it seemed to me that, nothing would pass *her* by.

Miss Grimshaw shook her head when we reached the kitchen. 'Well, that was time wasted if any could be.'

Master Jenkins looked out of sorts, and I did but wonder when he ever did seem *in* sorts. Perhaps he needed to find *something*. . . to make him truly well again.

Chapter Fifteen: A Fortuitous Event

I had plenty of work in the kitchen and about one-half hour later, as I cleaned out the large glass trifle serving bowl, what did I spy in the remains of the trifle, and covered by a good layer of egg custard? Sir John's cufflink, of course.

'Good Lord!' I stopped myself from saying any more, and quietly checked that a certain person had not heard my remark. Sarah, who was helping out by peeling vegetables across the table, looked over at me. When I put my finger to my lips. She nodded, she had seen me find it, and said nothing. I had to trust her.

This was something I realised I had no intention of letting Miss Grimshaw claim any credit for. With no wish to speak ill of her in any way, I admit I felt a little ashamed of myself. But if truth be known, only a tiny part ashamed. I smiled to myself at the thought.

I looked around and screwed a fist, hidden inside I took a careful hold of that slippery cufflink. I passed through the outside door and squinted into the sun as I crossed over to the water bucket. I plunged my fist in and opened it slightly as I vigorously moved it back and forth under the water. The result gave that thing of value a thorough clean and rinse. This I completed with a good shake to remove any water, a wipe on my pinafore brought up the shine of the gold.

This be special to me to see something of such value. I looked around and there be no one in sight. So, I held it towards the sun to check the obvious sparkle of the large stone, which I suspected to be a diamond, the like of which I had learned from various Sisters during my education, who had described the sparkle and fire in daylight. I soon realised that the value of this be something I could never possess. Whatever my thoughts on how lovely this item be, all I had in my mind, for never could I think otherwise, be that I should make it fit to present back to Sir John, without delay.

I said not a word, as I slowly mounted the stairs to attract no attention with the item well hidden in the folds of my pinafore dress. Once on the upper floor I could smell the attractive aroma of that special pipe tobacco from down the corridor, and it was easy to trace the origin. Indeed, I ran in, to my hearts delight, with my excitement gushing like a stream of honey, so happy did I feel. The Sir's smoking room be my heartfelt destination. Alone, he rested in his favourite armchair, surrounded by a blue cloud of tobacco smoke. I stood at the door and called in a low nervous voice.

'Sir John, I've found something I believe to be yours.'

He sprang out of his chair and advanced from the far side of the room in all haste, and nearly tripped over for his troubles, he staggered forward in anxious expectation towards the door, and held onto the table by the wall as he regained his balance. I offered my hand to him lest he need it. He stood for but a second, and took a deep breath.

'Bet, what, how?' He be truly lost for words.

The prize lay on the open palm of my hand as I offered it to Sir John.

He looked at me in wonder. . . then gazed down at it and uttered, as he picked it up, 'Oh my! I never thought I would ever see this again.'

He checked it over with his glasses on,' His gaze caught mine and for an instant, I noticed a changed expression on the Sir's face.

'My dear Bet, I don't know what to say. Where on earth did you find it?'

I spoke out as a proud person would do on a good day, 'Sir John, I had the good fortune to recover it from the bottom of the trifle dish, under a layer of custard.'

At this point Miss Emily appeared, and interrupted me. 'Sir John, wishes to say, 'Thank You.' Now return to your duty's young girl,'

Somewhat startled by her presence, I turned to see her pass me as she stormed into the room to take charge. 'John, you really must not be familiar with the staff,' she said. 'They will take liberties. You mark my words!'

I heard her say this as I turned to leave. I knew not where she had appeared from. I wanted only to be there in the room with Sir John. My first thought be that she would somehow disfavour me. This I soon dismissed. But these worries did follow me, I'm ashamed to admit. I wondered what other reason had she to be there. That fear cast such a fog of doubt for some brief time and spoiled the moment for me.

Sir John, had called me 'My dear Bet,' for the first time, and the finding of his cufflink I discovered be dear to my heart and did soothe that spoiled moment caused by the abrupt dismissal.

Mistress Emily's stay at Colesdale Hall lasted for three weeks. The first I heard of Miss Emily's departure date came from Miss Grimshaw. This brought me no surprise. 'I'll sigh from great relief on Friday, when I can finally relax a little, and not be on my toes all the time,' she said.

Despite my growing respect for Miss Emily I replied, 'Yes Miss Grimshaw, life will ease when we return to normal.' After all I spoke only the truth.

Our time during her stay was spent ensuring Miss Emily her every comfort. Sir John could be seen to constantly fuss about her, to make sure everything be to her perfect liking. On one occasion, I spotted a certain look upon her face which spoke to me of something else, apart from her obvious expectation to be waited upon head and foot. This and more I kept quiet about and discussed this subject with nobody.

I took it upon myself, although no right did I have, to pin a fresh posy of Sir John's flowers every day upon my white pinafore. These were forget-me-nots as a first choice. Fortunately, they lasted in the meadows for the duration of Miss Emily's stay. Would they dare to do anything else? I smiled at the thought. She missed this not. I saw her look but at first not a word did she say to me. This I believed to be Miss Emily following her own rule about not becoming familiar with the servants.

For my part, I spent a good amount of time every day placing around her portrait a fresh display of our best flowers. This was favourably commented upon by not only Miss Grimshaw and Sarah. But can you believe? Also, Miss Emily, who later spoke in my presence the day before she left, about, "the nice colourful flowers, which pleased me so." I noticed her left eyebrow rise while she said this, and took it as genuine approval. I smiled and curtsied, not able to look directly at her lest I stared at that black mole on her cheek.

At this time a gypsy camp had appeared outside the next village. This happened at a time when things started to disappear from our estate and area; only small things, but an annoyance to all. We were warned by a friendly neighbour not to buy anything they may try to sell us.

It was after the business with the cufflink, when a gipsy came to our door for some purpose; which be never revealed. Miss Emily saw him approach and rushed to the front door to answer it.

'I'll see to this,' she shouted, 'And watch the back door for more of these wretches.'

Miss Grimshaw heard and checked the rear where, sure enough, there stood for no good reason a poorly clothed woman in the back yard.

Such was the uproar as Miss Emily berated and chased this poor scruffy wretch off the property with the aid of her cane. Her cries of, 'Vagabond!' echoed around the estate to the amusement of all who were watching. The effect on the gypsy girl was immediate as I watched her turn and run to catch up with her partner.

Thomas came to the kitchen for a glass of lemon water. 'I kept my eye on that gypsy girl' he said. 'I didn't like the shifty manner she had. She looked far too interested in everything as she walked past the barn and stables. Just as well I be grooming the horses, because I fear she would have entered the buildings.'

Miss Emily, left us about a week after the event with the cufflink. Her leaving created a similar scene as during her, *'Royal,'* arrival. Thomas had cleaned and polished the Sir's coach and dressed himself in the smart clothing Sir John had bought for him. So a nicely presented coach and driver awaited Miss Emily.

I stood there, the last in line with the same smile upon my face. Miss Emily made her regal way to the line-up. This time I noticed she gave me a quick glance and, can you believe it? A nod, yes, a royal nod, as she charged by. I acknowledged with a bow of my head and curtsey towards my betters, as I would royalty. My belief was that she carried a lot of face to hide behind. With the coach already loaded with her trunks, she soon sat resplendent inside. We all waved her off, including Sir John.

It be on the next morn after Miss Emily's departure, that as I swept the hearth out to finish the fire, Sir John appeared. He indicated for me to carry on with my work, while he waited, then I arose and straightened my pinafore dress for all modesty, flicked a strand of hair off my face and turned to face him.

He waved his hand for me to sit on that red chair, and sat opposite again on his favourite chair.

'You made a good impression on Emily. I swear I know of no one else who has ever done that before,' His voice went soft.

'Well done.'

I may have looked a little surprised. Again, my tongue led the way.

'Sir John, your sister I do like, for I see only a kind soul, who if the circumstances allowed me. I would like to get to know. . . I mean, how she is truly.'

He looked at me and I could see he was thinking about something.

'Oh yes. . . uhm! I have this for you, a little thank you for your honesty. I haven't had chance to thank you properly.' Shyly he handed me a large bound volume.

I be as shocked as ever I could be. The Complete Works of Shakespeare. Never would I imagine a kitchen maid presented with such a book, or any book.

'Sir, I cannot accept this generous gift. This be more than I ever would dream of owning.'

'My dear Bet, the diamond in that cufflink is valuable, and has been in our family for three hundred years. It would be a big blow if I lost it. I will never wear them again. They are far too precious.'

He stared into the fire without seeing, as he gathered his thoughts.

'You are now nearly sixteen and I believe it be time to leave your work as a kitchen help.'

He paused, and turned to look at me.

I had time-a-plenty to worry and I knew I shouldn't, but the pause nearly killed me with anticipation and the fear grew in my belly. This be the way of Sir John. I knew he had thought a plenty about this subject, and trusted him only second to God. Eventually he started again:

'Bet, I want you to be my personal house keeper answerable only to me. You are to take charge of most matters concerning my living quarters. This includes the duties of the chamber maid who will work under you. Master Jenkins will continue to be my valet and in charge of the rest of the servants. This should ease the work on everyone.' He paused and said, 'I do hope this suits you. Your pay will rise to two shillings and six pence per week. You will have a nice room to yourself and wear a patterned pinafore as befits your new situation.'

I'm both shocked and delighted. This be five times my present wage and with a bedroom to myself. . . 'Oh Sir . . .' I started to say, but he interrupted me.

'It will be my pleasure to see more of you, to have your bright smile, um… yes. I must find another to take your place.' he said, as he stared into the fireplace again, 'And before I forget, if you need any help I'm always here.'

I left his Lordship's presence with delight at my new position. And was it fear I felt deep inside me, of what he nearly said?

He be after all a *man.* I felt most confused.

Miss Grimshaw caught my ear that same morn with her snippet of gossip.

'Did you know that Thomas has shown an interest in Sarah? I've only just heard.'

'And is Sarah, interested?' I asked.

'She takes her time; it would seem she be decent to me. But I'm too old to be fooled. She shakes and flusters when he be near. I imagine her heart is well made up!'

'They would make a nice couple,' Thinking aloud.

'Yes, I agree.'

'Uhm! I wonder? A germ of an idea took root in my mind.

Miss Grimshaw looked at me, 'Bet, what are you cooking up in that brain of yours?'

I smiled. She said nothing more, she was learning.

I did but wonder what she would say when she learned from Sir John about the changes. This I must say occupied my mind no small time during this short period. It was down to Sir John to tell everyone, and make the changes. I waited with almost my breath held.

Chapter Sixteen: Changing Times

July the year of the Lord 1738

At this time, I truly felt the charm of God's will as I penned these few lines in my diary.

We had not long to wait. In the afternoon Sir John gathered us all in the dining room where we formed a group all eager to hear about the changes so long promised.

He stood before us in his brown riding clothes, the ones he used for hunting. Freshly shaved, his face shiny with a balm the faint sweet smell of which did affect me so. He looked at ease as he took charge, like someone used to public speaking. In no hurry he scanned our faces and seemed to look at all of us in turn, a clever way to start a conversation I thought.

Now, did he look at Master Jenkins who stood to one side? I think not. Tis perhaps true that I own a fanciful perception. But if I be right and he did ignore him. . . I wonder? I be surely the only one to notice. Not even Master Jenkins noticed. I be most sure of that.

Sir John cleared his throat and spoke kindly, as he explained the changes he had made.

'I would like you all to know that I be most happy and proud of your work. Tis for this I desire to rearrange the staff, both to lower your work load and concentrate extra work on the upper floor.'

He turned to me, 'To this end I promote Bet, to be my personal housekeeper and answerable only to me. She be wasted with her abilities to read and write where she be now. Bet will take charge of most matters concerning my living quarters. This includes the duties of the chamber maid who will work under her. Master Jenkins will continue to be my valet and in charge of the rest of the servants. This should ease the work on everyone.' He paused again and added, 'This of course means we will employ another kitchen maid.'

Sir John rounded up his talk by thanking everyone for their efforts during Miss Emily's visit. I didn't know what to think at first when we heard that she described our service as being, 'more than comfortable.' Could this be bordering on a compliment? Was I right about her? Did my instincts describe her contradictory character correctly, I wonder?

After Sir John left us, I went over in my mind the words he used when he kindly explained the changes. His words were well chosen and most fair, although not everyone will be happy about the arrangements. I refer of course to Master Jenkins, who worried about the loss of some of his responsibility. Despite this he said little to Sir John. He mumbled about having a matter that required his attention and promptly left us.

I will speak more of him presently.

I stood entranced as my life be about to change. I thought with pride of my freshly brushed, and shiny brown hair, one half yard long which flowed with soft comfort over my shoulders like a moorland stream. Miss Grimshaw disagreed with hair this length in a kitchen maid, 'It should be short as your work demands.'

The first time she told me, I said, 'It be *my* hair to choose. As you know, I tie it back with a rag when appropriate in the kitchen.'

I did only but look at her the second time she approached me on this subject. My widened blue eyes, and raised eyebrows seemed to close the matter. Maybe this be a fault of mine for I know that a show of stubbornness be not unknown in my countenance.

Through the small handmade and recently leaded windowpanes, the noon sun beamed shafts of hazy, blue light, and amid the haze somehow there rode the beautiful smell of Sir John's pipe tobacco.

My new position as Sir John's personal housekeeper I knew would turn out to bear no resemblance to my former position. Of this fact I be not wrong. From the beginning I charged myself to help Sir John as he required and so far, as I be able. I knew I had much more to learn and I threw myself into this new position with all my strength and a young woman's guile. Could this be me, Betty May, the kitchen waif? I told myself I must still be the same person. This I made clear to all I conversed with.

Sarah who be the main one affected by the changes, sported a big grin as she spoke. 'This be what I came to work for, and not to be looking behind me all the time. Tis almost like a new manner of service. How I be so pleased for you, Bet, and now I work for you. For me, this be surely heaven-sent.' She gave me a look which said everything without a wrong word uttered.

'Thank you, Sarah.' I felt touched by her sincerity and pleased to be able to improve her time in service, 'You know I be just the same Bet as before, 'I said. 'This idea be Sir John's, to make everything easier for us all, and ensure the smooth running of this house.'

Miss Grimshaw, at the first opportunity, took me to one side to converse with me after Sir John's impressive speech. 'So Bet, you have done well for an age of barely sixteen. I confess I be most surprised; this be not expected at all. How did you manage to do it?' She gave me a look I truly did not deserve.

'I can tell you now,' I said 'to put out of your mind any ideas you have in your head. You know where I came from. One of the last things my dear mother made me promise, be not to not take the same road as her and to be careful on whom I set my heart. So, I took much heed of what happened to her, even though she did little wrong, except in choosing the wrong man. The effect on her and my life may be considered unfair. So, you know I'll never, ever, take that road.'

'But your age and the position you hold, this be most irregular, don't you think?'

She didn't seem convinced. I awaited such a response from her; because I knew best how to deal with this situation, one I felt I had awaited all my life.

'Miss Grimshaw,' I said, 'it be only natural for Sir John, to want his house to be run in the best way. He feels the need to have more labour to ease the work on everyone.' I took the time to let this sink in, 'As you know I can read and write, so like he said, '" I be wasted as a kitchen maid of the lowest rank," I expect you to say nothing to Master Jenkins about all this. And finally, you are safe in your position here. As you know, I don't lie.'

Miss Grimshaw stood there and nodded as she thought over what I had said. I knew there be some envy in her discourse. With no harm in her, I had let my tongue soothe her worries and I heard no more from her about this matter.

Later, I did notice a certain reaction from Miss Grimshaw when she found out that I had the bedroom next door to her. It will no doubt give her a reason and subject to gossip about. This I ignored.

Chapter Seventeen:

I Have a Word with Master Jenkins

It was the next day when Sir John spoke with me while I busied myself with some chores on the second floor. He caught me by surprise and I missed some of his words.

'Dear Bet, I . . . asham . . . of . . . yself for I listened to what Miss Grimshaw said to you. This came up the dumb waiter where the door remained open.' He looked guilty, there be no denying it.

'Yes, I did but listen,' he continued, 'and this caused no ill in any way, for now I understand you more and have enormous respect for you in ways you may have yet to learn. Please believe me, this be important to me.'

I felt embarrassment in no small amount. For Sir John to be privy to a natural answer concerning my new position, and personal to me, did indeed cause me shock, I knew I must attempt to understand Sir John's dilemma.

With a mind to keep an even course, I said, 'There be no harm there, Sir John. You could only hear what be true, as I explained to Miss Grimshaw.'

With but a second's thought I gave Sir John one of my

beguiling smiles I had practised in the great hall looking glass; when no one watched of course, for so would I be embarrassed if it were otherwise. I tried to act past my age and felt far from being the confident, grown woman I wished to portray and, tis my belief I may have looked a little shy. At the time I was sure he noticed my unease.

Sir John said no more and indicated for me to follow him, and led me to my room. I had my few possessions with me; these included, of course, my treasured book and of course my diary. A bedroom with a window and all to myself - this was more than I could ever have hoped for. I felt most unworthy and expressed myself so to Sir John but I soon found out that he would not listen to my doubts of my deserving. It was then that he cut me off like before. Perhaps there was something there for me to learn.

'My dear Bet," he said 'I offer you no more than you have earned. If any debt is owed, it be mine. You have been a good influence to all around you, and your honesty and good cheer are worth more to me. . . Ahem! I had Sarah build a fire yesterday, and today, to make sure your room be aired. I have some things of Marie I must sort. Perhaps. . .'

I felt I could answer in the positive to Sir John, without being forward, for never, would I want to appear so, 'If the kind Sir would like help, in the assortment of any items, then I am at your summons.'

'No, when I think about it, you have more than enough to occupy yourself for now. Don't forget I wish to help you in any problem you may encounter, large or small; anything at all. This be a new position for you, and most important to me it is that you enjoy it and have nothing but the least of problems.'

When he left me, his words regarding the room filled my mind with thoughts and ideas. I realised my whole world had changed when I entered service at Colesdale; this was now my new life and I continued to grow into it. At times like this I looked back and wished my dear mother could see me now with a room to myself. I was sure she would have been proud of her only child. I had no right to thoughts that reached beyond this. . . But perhaps a certain person? Nay! How could I think so? Again, that fear I do so feel about *men.* This was the reason for my need of help from the 'Lord.' I still prayed daily with devotion.

With much still to learn, I determined at this time to listen and be careful with my decisions, and to keep a hold of my tongue, or at least try to. I had only just received my new pinafore, which suited me and fitted well. I couldn't help as I gazed into the looking glass at myself.

A warm glow spread about me, as I unpacked the few things I possessed into the top drawer of the chest of drawers. It was then I realised how few clothes I had to my name. I had only use for the top one of the four drawers. This may sound strange but it troubled me not, for I enjoyed such joyful contentment for almost the first time in my life, to have a room of my own. I had but scarce time to fulfil my needs of joyful expectation as I explored the room's little secrets.

A loud knock rapped against my door. I jumped; this bothered me no small amount, for who would knock so? I was soon to find out.

Before I could ask who, it be, the door flew open. It caused me no small concern when without my permission, in walked Master Jenkins.

I felt concerned and annoyed, I threw back my hair away from my face, and flashed my eyes as I turned towards him, 'And what gives you the right to charge into my room like this?' I demanded. I knew he was clearly in the wrong. This forced me to speak out, I cared not how I sounded and my irritation must have carried in my voice.

After a pause he answered, 'No one else complains.'

He sounded defensive. This was the first time I had heard this tone from him. Was this weakness, I wondered.

'Look, in future you wait till I open the door,' I said, staring at him, 'Yes?'

He chose not to answer, so I repeated, 'You wait in future. . .

Yes?'

To my mild surprise, with some reluctance, he nodded.

'Now what brings you here?'

'This new change means that you see to all that takes place above the ground floor. I do not like it one bit.'

I believe in his mind I be still that waif that entered service at age thirteen.

'No! No! No!' I answered with some heat. 'You have this wrong. I am responsible for the smooth running of his living area, with only Sarah under my control. You are still his valet. We can work it out who serves Sir John his food. It can change with circumstances between Miss Grimshaw, yourself, or even me. Surely you can see how much easier it will be for us all when we engage another kitchen maid?' I watched him closely.

Master Jenkins mumbled something and without a further word left my room. I noticed he shut the door quietly. This showed he be under control. It pleased me to think I had been able to override his natural temper. It seemed he truly found it distasteful to converse with me. It was down to him to adapt to any new situation.

I sighed and ran over in my mind my new situation. I started to sing a hymn in a low voice as I carried on with arranging my very first bedroom. This be my day, a happy moment in my life. Nothing, and certainly not even Master Jenkins, could spoil this. I decided to gather and arrange some flowers to grace my bedroom. I noticed earlier that Sir John had placed a glass vase upon the chest of drawers. This could only be for me, I decided. How thoughtful of him!

So it be, when I went out to the garden to select a bunch of wildflowers, I did by chance come across Thomas who be taking a little sun, while lying against a bank with his head rested against his interlocking fingers. He smiled as I approached,

'I've not been here all day. Case you wonder,' he said with a cheeky look about him.

'Thomas, your work is to the satisfaction of Sir John, and no responsibility do I have over you,' I replied as I sat down close by on a tree stump. 'A little bird told me about you and Sarah,' I added, thinking we be friends enough to talk like this.

He squinted against the sun as he spoke, 'I be lost for ideas of how to became acquainted with her and perhaps become her friend. I feel I cannot talk to her like I can with you,' He looked lost.

I had no realisation before now of any feelings he might have for me. I merely regarded him as a friend with whom I could engage in converse. I had no desire for this to go further. Then I remembered something. 'Would you like to hear what I suggest?' I asked.

'Of course, Bet, I don't mind.'

'I've seen her on the occasion with a bible in her hand; it must be hers for I know of no other one she could use. This indicates to me her strong belief in God. So perhaps it may be an idea for you to take an interest and perhaps she will accompany you to Church on Sunday.' I looked at him.

He unclasped his hands, sat up, and gave me a look of the sort he should save for Sarah.

Not quite the response I wanted. I felt protected by my woman's instinct, which guided me. He might be after-all my friend, but he still be a man. With that I took my leave.

My early days were a distant memory as I reflected on my present position. It be shortly after my appointment that Sir John approached me when I was on my own and spoke. 'Well Bet, I've seen nothing but harmony in the working of this household. How is young Alice the new pantry maid coming on?'

'Though this be Master Jenkins responsibility, I will say in the week she's been with us, she seems to be up to the work as far as I can tell.'

Although not asked, I arranged with a somewhat reluctant Master Jenkins a new work routine of more convenience to Sir John. I must confess at the time; I did greatly worry for his good grace. After all, I had to keep reminding myself, who I was. I need not have felt such concern; Sir John showed his satisfaction by his frequent encouragement and advice.

It was about this time when Sir John had to go on buiseness to London. He said that he would be away for ten days and looked concerned for me. I felt I was able to free him from any worries about me, by pointing out that Thomas would be with us and not driving the coach. We all knew that Thomas would look after us if need be.

Chapter Eighteen: A Dire Situation

It was one morn, only a day or two after Sir John caught the coach to London, when Sarah my chamber maid and I were in the linen room. I made it my duty to replace some of Sir John's linen so old, grey and near to holes it be. It is then that I noticed she be quiet and worried looking.

'Sarah I must ask, is everything alright between you and Thomas?'

It was shortly after I spoke to Thomas about his interest in Sarah. Therefore, it came to mind that he might have said something to her by now. 'Forgive me,' I continued, 'I have no wish to be nosey. It's perhaps none of my business, only that you seem so sad this morn. I do wonder if there be anything I can do?' I looked at her and felt her sorrow. She looked unsure of herself. I only wondered as her tears started to flow.

'Does he not speak to you?' I asked in a cautious fashion. At last, a reaction.

'Oh! We talk when able and have a few moments. But it be what he has just told me this morn. This be a story of some length to be told correctly.'

This impressed me that she did gather her thoughts so. When the time was revealed for this private discourse, although I heard not the reason so far, I used my instinct and judged correctly.

'Then let us speak together now in private,' I closed the door to the small linen room behind us and waved my hand towards a cane chest we used for linen storage to indicate her to sit upon it. I sat upon another one next to her. I realised her need for private discourse be of some importance to her, and I allowed a short pause, so she could explain her thoughts. From the beginning, she had always regarded me more as her friend, as indeed I would wish.

'So, speak to me, Sarah.'

Her need be so great to tell me that she spoke with uncommon speed, which made it necessary for me to ask her to speak slowly. It was only then, that I realised she did speak of Thomas Greene our coachman and the reason for his melancholy. Miss Grimshaw who, earlier this morning, had gossiped and talked of this matter for a good twenty minutes, had noticed this about him.

'His brother, Peter, is due to be tried on the next quarter day assizes in York, next month,' said Sally, slowing down in her speech.

'May I enquire the reason?'

'He be accused of stealing a saddle from his master's stable.'

'Thomas swears his brother would never, ever, do such a

thing.'

'And where did this take place?' I asked, my interest now aroused.

'But some five miles away in Stansfield farm near Hinton village,'

'And what be the outcome, Sarah?'

'I believe you must ask Thomas about the details, because he be too distressed when he spoke to me about Peter.'

I could understand the distress and the reason why this girl, quiet and retiring though she be, would indeed feel too upset to relate the matter further to me, even in private. Therefore, I resolved myself to find out more about this tragic situation. Later in the day, I took the liberty to talk in private with Thomas.

'Sarah has told me of your dreadful plight. What pray, may I ask, is the situation with your brother?'

'Oh Bet! My brother be falsely accused of theft. I spoke to him and I know him to be the most honest of men. As you know, he will be hung if found guilty.' He gulped, and bravely continued, 'While in York, after meeting my brother, I happened by chance to have the misfortune to see the convicted murderer, Robin Teller. . . *hanged*. . . Not a pleasant sight, and one which I be sure will haunt me for life. This offence to our eyes sickened my stomach and terrified my mind. A large crowd gathered there. This included his family who continued to shout his innocence, just feet away from the scaffold. T'were all so terrible to behold,' He paused. . . 'This Robin Teller struggled and screamed to the end. It took three strong men to hold him while the executioner slipped the rope around his neck. He fell a good distance and danced an awful dance at the end of the rope for so long. The executioner, for the price of a silver shilling thrown by Robin Teller's brother, jumped down, grabbed the macabre, dancing, puppet like figure by his legs, and pulled down hard. A loud crack indicated his neck had been broken and he moved no more. The smell of death pervaded the area. A loud wailing broke out in the crowd. The hangman, a cruel and stupid man, spoke out in a loud voice, 'Be a good strong neck that one, I should have charged a florin,' He said with a laugh, 'Could have put my back out.' His loud laughter be nearly (and by rights should have been) his downfall, for I heard a man's desperate cry 'With the help of the Lord and all that be holy. . .I'll get. . . You... you monster!'

A banshee yell of terror rang out as if from some fiend from the very depths of Hell. The hangman in his cowardly manner, raised his hands in defeat. At this very moment the brother launched himself at him and with his bare hands did his best to dis-assemble him, but fortunately for the hangman, his gristle and sinew held his body together. Thus, he barely escaped with his life, such was his poor state. A squad of grenadiers rescued him, with his clothing in tatters and covered in his own blood. The brother could be heard to shout out, 'For the love of God, someone pass me a knife so I can silence this monster,'

It was to the executioner's undeserved good fortune that no one did. The brother be held in jail and due to be tried before the assizes for an attack on a hangman carrying out the King's command, and he will without doubt end up like his brother Robin. . . hanged!' Thomas added with a whisper, 'Next to mine.'

'I'll explain this to Sir John because he needs to know,'

We all liked Thomas, and it be most sad to see him so distraught.

Once again, my tongue took control, and inside I shook like one of Sir John's favourite, giant jellies Miss Grimshaw, so enjoyed making. Off guard be I now, when Thomas kissed me on the cheek. I felt his tears.

'You are such a kind- hearted lady and only sixteen years old,'

He hid his tears and hurried away. Never before had I been called a lady, such an impostor be I.

Without a single good idea of how to approach Sir John, I worried so. Today be Monday, and he be due back on the coach to York on Wednesday, where Thomas will pick him up in his own coach and driven back to Colesdale. So, I had two days to work out how to approach him. This gave me time a plenty to doubt myself, as I most surely did. Worry be so like a poison to my insides, though I be learning that perhaps I can trust my tongue. Yet this be no medicine for my soul. I only want to perform for the best before Sir John, and to the benefit of Thomas.

Sir John arrived back on time after attending to his varied business in London. I couldn't help but notice how he beamed with pleasure, his eyes bright, with a sunny smile which stayed in place and a carefree manner I'd not seen in him before. I was soon to learn the reason for his exuberant countenance.

'Dear Bet, Sir Robert Walpole, an acquaintance of mine, took me to the Royal Court of King George II in London. You will never believe this, but he introduced me to the King who spoke to me and took note of my name. I understand that he always remembers names. This could be of good use in the future.'

'Oh, Sir how wonderful!' I replied. I could but only imagine the scene. This certainly was not a good moment to approach Sir John about the important matter, so I left it for the time being.

Later, while I laid out the dinner service, selfishly concerned about the important matter and how to approach Sir John, I be so lost in thought that I heard not his footsteps as he came behind me into the room.

'Come on, my dear Bet, let's have it, I always know when something troubles you.'

I jumped. . . and rapidly recovered my dignity, 'Oh, Sir John it's about Thomas!' I blurted out. 'Go on then, Bet. . . Let us hear it!'

He listened intently, as I explained to him all the details regarding the plight of Thomas's brother, Peter.

'I'll go and have a word with him now, to see if there be anything I can do.'

Later we heard a flurry of activity in the stable yard as Thomas checked over and bedded down the horses. Sir John had ordered his carriage made ready for an eight o'clock departure the next morn. I was sat with Miss Grimshaw by the kitchen range as we sewed the seams of our new, warm, winter undergarments with linen supplied by the local milliner.

'This be a wonder that Sir John be willing to help Thomas's brother whom he has never met.' Miss Grimshaw looked at me. She had heard about the plight of Thomas who was most open about it.

'No, I find this to be expected of the Kind Sir. Though of course it be a wonderful thing he do. I only hope the Lord helps, and he wins the day. The thought of what could happen to Thomas's brother grieves me so.'

'Yes Bet, that was what I meant to say.'

At that moment Sir John approached me, 'Bet, I'm going with Thomas tomorrow morning to York. We'll be gone for a few days. I don't know how long it'll take to find a cure for this problem so dire.' He said nothing more because of the presence of Miss Grimshaw.

'Yes, Sir John. Have no worries. . .' Master Jenkins appeared at the back door and interrupted me.

'You know Sir John, that you can depend on me, whenever you go on a journey.'

'Er, yes. . . of course,' he said, and he turned to walk up the stairs.

Sir John, had hesitated. I did so wonder why?

Master Jenkins gave us both a questioning look; which we ignored. We left him in the dark, as regards the business of Sir John. He would find out in good time.

Next morn I watched them leave. Thomas drove, as they headed for York. I could but wonder and hope what would come out of all this, 'God Willing!'

It was sometime later afore Thomas be able to relate to me how Sir John questioned him closely about his brother Peter and decided on the spot to try and help.

Dusk descended and I heard the clip clop of the horse's hooves on the dry ground. Sir John returned to his chamber to freshen up. In the meantime, I busied myself and laid the table to Sir John's liking. I had noticed that he liked a nice apple and a short knife by his plate. These and a few details I did see to as I waited.

Master Jenkins, on his way to bring Sir John's dinner from the kitchen, had cause to pass me, Whereupon he shook his head as he looked slyly at me.

'Master Jenkins, what?. . .' my words drifted into the ether as he charged down the steps. I followed him down into the kitchen, with my tongue ready to take over. I stood and watched, with a smile upon my face, a failing of mine. 'Master Jenkins,' I said. 'I see you are dis-pleasured in some way. 'Am I the cause? If this be so, I wish to know.'

'I cannot believe my eyes; you should not be involving Sir John in the affairs of the staff! I've never seen the likes of this before in service, never!'

'Well, Master Jenkins, with all due humility wipe your eyes, because it happens afore you now.'

A deeply unpleasant sight presented itself. He changed in an instant afore me to a deep red of face, beads of sweat littering his brow like frozen rain on a winter's window. Worst of all, I watched as his eyes roll out of sight. His pupils were now large with rage. He glared at me like some wild beast cheated out of its prey. I felt a distinct warning in my belly, fear perhaps. I be after all just a feeble young woman of no great strength.

'Is the kind Master going to chain me again?' I asked 'Does he have some reason to silence me, for so as I may deserve?'

I truly knew not why I said these things. Miss Grimshaw, who had listened to the conversation added, to try and calm the situation. 'Tis a good thing that Bet did, isn't it Master Jenkins?'

He took a long look at her, and came to a realisation. With nothing more to say he turned tail and stormed out of the kitchen. This time he slammed the door. This pleased me so, but I knew this would not to be the end to the matter.

'Just as well I be here, what say you Bet?' Miss Grimshaw remarked.

Chapter Nineteen: Sir John's Intervention

March the year of the Lord 1742.

Sir John had kindly helped as I shall reveal. My diary be opened and my pen at the ready, with no small concern for Thomas Greene and his brother Peter, as do I write these notes. How thankful and fortunate be I, to be able not just to write this account, but to report that what followed be the facts as I know them.

Before I continue, I must first report the situation as regards Master Jenkins.

At this time while Sir John had gone away to a meeting, a problem of a different nature showed its face. This pleased me not, for Sir John had enough problems to occupy him. I did so want to solve this before his return.

Dear Sarah came to me again; I call her 'dear' because of her nature. She is such a sweet, retiring girl, with a generous heart and thoughts for others.

'I.. . I, don't want to t.. . trouble you Bet,' she said, staring down at the floor.

I couldn't help but notice the red eyes and the unhappy looking countenance of this tortured young woman. So, I waited for her with a patience which I admit to still be only now, learning.

'I. . . I must ask to be a. . . allowed to leave my work. . . I want to leave, Bet.'

'Oh, my dear Sarah, what has driven you to this? I thought that you were happy here?' I almost felt that a hug be needed. Then I remembered my position.

'I'm too imperfect to work my time here.'

This gave me a clue. Imperfect? (I thought fast). 'No one be perfect here.' I replied, 'Not I, nor Sir John. Not Master Jenkins.' I looked at her.

Call it something, perhaps a female intuition. For a moment, I let her relax a little, she be so tense in her bearing.

'Tell me truthfully, Sarah. What did Master Jenkins say to you? I must know.' I took my time, 'Before you do, let me tell you, my thoughts. If this problem be not resolved, then I will join you and we shall leave Colesdale Hall together,' I smiled at her, such be my confidence in Sir John.

Eventually I managed to tease it all out of her.

Because she was my charge and working only for me, I wondered at first if I had given her reason to leave. My worry was ill founded. She gave me the reason after a little more, gentle discourse and kindly persuasion. Master Jenkins had been teasing her constantly and made personal comments about her speech impediment (brought out only by his personal comments). I tried to put her mind to rest and promised to find a remedy for the problem, so unhappy did I feel for her. Though to be honest I was far from sure how this could all be achieved. I had much to learn. My discourse seemed to work with Sarah and I could see her spirits had lifted when I left her to carry on with her work.

I immediately made for Master Jenkins with no small feelings in my belly, of something; I wonder, could it be dread?

I found him in the backyard where an unhappy Jess the cocker spaniel whined at his rough ministrations, as he scrubbed her with a none too soft brush. Miss Grimshaw was also nearby as she scrubbed the outside step, prior to donkey stoning it. I found no enjoyment and was forced to let my tongue have its way as follows. I fear I spoke loud against all advice from the nuns in the distant past. But this be a situation that required strength. I almost laughed, *STRENGTH*, in my weak frame?

'Master Jenkins, I see you have found it fitting to comment in an unfavourable way about Sarah, who I may remind you, rests under my charge. If it be necessary to express any opinion about her, I would ask you to kindly say it to me.'

'What! What! Well bless my soul, I have a jumped-up scullery maid who has made demands of me!'

Puce of face, he advanced towards me. I stood firm and with

149

weak knees held my ground. Again, I be aware of my slight build, little more than a mere child against this large bully.

'Master Jenkins, we won't have any of that,' warned Miss Grimshaw.

'Mind your own business. This matter doesn't concern you.'

This gave me an idea of how to proceed, having seen him far too often in the Sir's drinks larder. 'Master Jenkins,' I said. 'I do wonder as other people might, of the cause for that red glow upon your face.' By this time, I had no small fear of him, even though I knew I was right.

'What do you mean by that. . .Wench?'

'My position be personal housekeeper to Sir John, 'Wench' be an incorrect title. As regards your red face this would be for Sir John to remedy as fit and proper.'

I did wonder if I had gone too far. Master Jenkins advanced further towards me and again I didn't move. He looked down at me, his face inches from my mine. I could smell that horrible smell again of stale brandy.

'It would cause more disadvantage to you than to me, truly Master Jenkins,' I said.

That was enough. To my considerable relief, after a few long moments, he turned around, hesitated, then walked away.

I realised that this be an unsatisfactory state of affairs and Sir John must be made aware of Master Jenkins' behaviour at the earliest opportunity.

Chapter Twenty: Sir John Returns

Sir John arrived later that day accompanied by that familiar sound, as the coach and two horses, crunched their way down the gravel- covered drive up to the front door. I heard his instructions to Thomas regarding the horses. I thought the time might be ideal to approach him as he walked towards his private room. He carried a small bag and some other papers.

At an earlier date I would never be so forward to Sir John: now with certain responsibilities, I did feel a need to be the first to know, though still if truth be known, I did for some reason shiver some, as if cold. I felt stupid with that feeling in the pit of my stomach, and my need to be careful with him. So, I spoke out. 'Sir John, how did the journey turn out, be there a good result? I ask so I may answer anything asked of me.'

He looked somehow dazed as he turned to me.

'Dear Bet, the result turned out to be satisfactory but I cannot load you with the details just at the moment. Best later at a more convenient time,' He nodded his encouragement with raised eyebrows. Did he mean to ask me if I minded? As if I would!

I could tell now he was somewhat tired, or out of sorts. His eyes be red, and I guessed due to the travel and the movement of the coach.

'Of course, Sir John, I had Sarah use the warming pan in your bed to make sure it be well aired for you. I'll bring you a cup of hot sugared milk if you so desire?'

'Er, yes Bet, that would be nice.'

In the kitchen I took the liberty to ask Miss Grimshaw to cut a generous slice of her mixed fruit cake. This I left with his drink on his breakfast table in the day room.

There be something I wanted to do before I went to my bed. Thomas, I knew would be found in the stable, where he always spent time with the horses after a trip. He took care and loved them as if his own. I know this from what I witness by the day

"I could never find a better stable boy to look after my horses. He be a natural, if ever I did espy one." Sir John confided with me, in the recent past.

Thomas spotted me as I walked across the moonlit yard and spoke out to me from the door of the candle lit stable.

'Ah! Bet, nice to see you, has perchance Sir John enlightened you regarding the facts about what happened in York?'

'Tis good to see you well, he did tell me that the result be satisfactory, but no more until at a more convenient time.'

'Yes, well I be overwhelmed by what the kind Sir has done for Peter, who I assure you will never permit a bad word said against him. It's not my place to explain the details, that be, for the kind Sir.

I asked him no more, for I had no desire to be a nuisance.

So, the next morn I made myself visible to Sir John so as to remind him about my need for converse. Always naturally modest about his efforts, he needed encouragement on more than one occasion, before I understood the whole story. Sometime after breakfast he called me into his morning room. where I sat on my chair facing him, I do call it *my chair* for there were many times now I used it so. Sir John had a small occasional table he used when writing or reading sheets of script. Upon this he had a neat pile of paperwork; work he was dealing with. By the length of his description, he showed how he wanted me to know the details. I sat and listened.

'Thomas drove my coach and just the two of us on our journey to York. We made good time on the sun hardened roads. A peasant did warn us of outlaws in Wayfast Forest, and made reference to some trouble there recently. This be some ten miles from York. We encountered a band of lepers with mainly pikes with which they threatened us with. This called for the judicious use of the whip by Thomas and a discharge of my pistol.

I suspected these lepers came from the nearby Blackthorn Abbey where they were supposed to be welcome. I confess I didn't understand their desperate act, to try and hold up the coach. I had no mind to report these wretches when we arrived in York.'

*'They required help and medicines for their physical state and were pitiful, down to a man. I discharged the pistol into the air above their heads. This allowed our escape. I also tossed them a silver crow*n. *I could see a scramble for it as Thomas drove the coach at top speed away from these outlaws.'*

Sir John stopped to collect his thoughts and looked a little sheepish.

'Ah Bet, forgive me, of course you know the news in York be good and I shall try to describe it for you now.'

I feigned a relieved and sympathetic countenance to help him find the words. For I be most anxious to hear how Sir John had saved the life of Peter, from so foul of fate as a hanging.

Sir John continued, 'Because of our problem on the road going to York, we were late arriving.' Sir John was striving to recall the event in detail. 'We made a stop, for but a few minutes, to water the horses at the White Horse Inn, conveniently situated but a few miles North East and well past Wayfast Forest. I must admit that I be under the weather due to the travel motion of the carriage. So once there, Thomas suggested I try a restorative French brandy for which this Inn be well known, so for this reason I agreed. And I quickly downed a gill of this brandy, taken with water of course, for the first time in my life while traveling. I found as Thomas declared it would, that the French spirit indeed made me feel better. He who suggested this, would only himself accept but a small ale, for which I assuredly be grateful, seeing as it lay in his charge to drive our coach and horses. We rode over roads and lanes and a hundred potholes, thankfully mostly dried out after these weeks of sunny weather.

We journeyed past and through a hundred green fields, on our approach to York. It was late that afternoon, with the bright sun low on the horizon, beams of light streaming into our eyes as we travelled on. At the end of the journey, it caught us by surprise. . .when before us stood a substantial Tudor Coaching House. The sign indicated The Castle Inn, which be our lodgings for the night.

The Landlord was a jovial, rotund man who had a joke for almost everything. He offered us food and drink as required, so by the time we bedded the horses down, had sustenance and played a game of skittles, for a farthing wager, it was time for sleep, so worn out did I feel.'

Sir John continued with his description of events. I could tell he enjoyed relating them to me.

'After some delay I managed to contact the Magistrate, a Mr J.H. Fisk. Special permission was needed for my visit and I had to insist that Thomas be with me to interview Peter. I own up to the fact that I declared I had the King's ear and mentioned a couple of names. I made no reference to any possible plea of innocence for it be likely, in that case, we would have been refused entry.

Eventually we were granted access and the jailer I took an instant dislike to. My thoughts were that he should be an inmate himself, inside the dungeons, and not the jailer on the outside; such wretched circumstances we found for these unfortunates contained within the walls. It was in poor comfort that we eventually found Peter, who was sat on the cell floor with three other men, each one chained separately to the wall, all in abject misery, in a cold, dirty, and, rat infested dungeon. His appreciation for the bread and meat we gave him be all too obvious in his hurried eating. I insisted he take my overcoat for, in his present circumstance, his need be much greater than mine.

I had to wait some small time till he felt ready to answer my questions, so bad was his health by this time. It warmed my heart to see the good that a few mouthfuls of good food did before my eyes. In but an hour or two's time, I became able to see how the circumstances had conspired against Peter, the stableman and to no genuine discredit on his behalf.

From my extensive questions, I learned during this discourse, that on that fateful evening after dinner, Peter had set out for his regular evening walk. As he passed through the farm, he naturally checked as he always did that all be in order, and noticed with some alarm; a certain door ajar. This concerned him because it was the saddle and tackle store for which he was responsible. He knew right away that something was most wrong. A quick look inside confirmed his suspicions. An empty space on the rough wooden shelf indicated, that a saddle had to be missing.'

As I wrote this later into my diary, I could still see the sincerity in Sir John's eyes, as he continued with his account of the past few days.

'*A worried Peter made his way through the muddy yard towards the fields, where he noticed a gate pulled shut but not properly locked with the cross bar. He passed through the gate, charged forth, and before long could make out in the distance the figure of a small man as he carried a heavy load. When he had made up some distance and stood two or three hundred paces away. Peter shouted forth, "Stop thief," and gave chase across the third field. He ran hard despite the boggy areas, over and around thistles. He increased his speed as he gained ground and shouted loud again.*'

'Stop thief.'

'When Peter had made up more ground and could make out

the thief's features, the man dropped the saddle to the ground, and drew a knife. He shouted back and threatened to stab Peter if he came any closer; then this badly clothed man with a grey ponytail disappeared through a hedge. Peter ran forward, picked up the saddle and proceeded to run at a slow pace back in the direction he had just come. A few minutes later the gamekeeper, Master Denning, surprised Peter as he climbed a fence to cross the last field. Out of breath all Peter could gasp was, "He got away," and pointed to a gap in the he hedge which bordered that distant field.

"Yes, a likely tale indeed," said Master Denning in reply.

Peter said that he tried to convince Master Denning of the true circumstances, but could not get him to understand. He was stubborn in his opinion of what had occurred.

'So, from what I could gather by this time as described by Peter, our would-be thief could have travelled half a mile by this time, and be well out of sight.

Peter was then accused of attempted theft and made the subject of a citizen arrest.'

I well remember the intensity of Sir John's account because at this point, he was interrupted. I had to check a linen delivery; a matter which required instant attention. When I returned minutes later, I waited for him while he filled up his pipe, and lit it with a taper from the fire. He sucked on the pipe and blew the smoke in rings upwards in the direction of the ceiling. For some reason I found this slightly amusing and suppressed a smile. He stopped immediately coughed and then continued his account:

'By now Peter's innocence seemed obvious to me, so we made haste and Thomas drove us at top speed to enable me to make further enquiries at the estate where Peter worked. We had the help of the owner, a Mr Biddle, who stated to me, "This be a sad time indeed, and all for the sake of a saddle and an old one at that!"

He was gracious enough to attend and witness the proceedings and also called in Master Denning, (who had no choice in the matter though he looked most uncomfortable) to come over and to attend us. He was the only witness who saw Peter as he carried the saddle. And stated to me.'

'There be no doubt in my mind that Peter was the thief,' he declared. ''I caught him with the saddle after all!' With his voiced raised so, he was most vocal about the matter.

When I questioned him further, Master Denning admitted that Peter made no attempt to escape; he carried only the saddle and walked towards him when apprehended, and not away from him.'

Sir John had a habit of halting a conversation as he gathered his thoughts, this had me willing him to continue which eventually he did.

'By now I had a good idea of what had happened. We followed the steps of Peter with the guidance of Master Denning, to the fence at the first field. From there we continued to the second field which again had an easy pass border, then on to the third field where we found a hole in the hawthorn hedge at the far side that a man could easily pass through. When I examined it, I grabbed at something which could be seen sticking out of the bush. It turned out to be a riding crop and identified by Mr Biddle as his property. This find be also witnessed by Master Denning and established (in my mind) Peter's account of events as being correct. Further enquiries revealed that at the time there be a Gypsy camp just one half a mile away, beyond the estate.'

Master Denning's face told it all,' as he blurted out, 'Oh my! Well, he must have dropped it somehow and returned when he saw me.'

So, I asked him, 'Do you actually believe that Peter ran back across two fields towards you, just because he saw you?' I told him right to his face, 'I was not to be having that. . . Peter, did what any honest person would do and returned Mr Biddle's saddle as soon as he was able. Why don't you admit you made a mistake, and save the poor boy's life?' I pressed him hard upon this point, 'Well?'

I noticed that Mr Biddle nodded in agreement, held up his hand as he considered for a second or two, and announced, "Master Denning you be wrong here, I can see that plainly now. You must reconsider, for all that be right in this world. Do you wish to send a poor innocent boy to the gallows and an early death?" He be plainly convinced by now of Peter's innocence.

Master Denning took a long look at Mr Biddle. I could see his inner conflict as he struggled to come to terms with this new insight into what he thought he had witnessed.

He displayed some honesty as he replied, "Yes. . .Ahem. . .I know what I thought at the time. And now I believe I be wrong. I don't know what to say."

I must admit he looked shocked. It would seem that he was a man who had perhaps come to a first conclusion far too quickly. I took the opinion he seemed at least honest. When I pressed him, he did agree to travel with us back to York and present a retraction on the grounds that he was mistaken. I promised to help him write a simple statement. I also promised him there would be no trouble over this, because it was just an easily made mistake. I noticed his pale face and almost felt sorry for him.'

So back we went straight to York gaol. It was a Tuesday night and any protests were silenced by the firkin of ale I reluctantly left for the jailers.

'Once there I questioned Peter again in prison, regarding the rest of the missing riding tackle. He was at a loss to answer this question, being under the impression that only the saddle had been taken. Peter's intention had been to return the saddle to the store and then to inform Mr Biddle so as to cause him little worry.

The only course of action now, was the need for a representation to be made to the Magistrate Mr J H Fisk, where I could use my influence and the potential interest of our Sovereign (a slight exaggeration) to procure the release due to wrongful arrest, of the prisoner, Peter Greene.

This we did the next day, and once the Magistrate was acquainted with the full facts and the retraction by Master Denning, in writing; stated in his own words. 'This poor man had the welfare of his master at heart and we repaid him thus.'

'To his immense relief Peter was released the next day. I noted that Mr Biddle met him with an apology and the offer of further employment. I suggested that Peter upon his return, be given a full one gill measure of fine port with an egg and a portion of best pork and fat every day until such time that good health be restored. When Peter left with Mr Biddle and Master Denning. I had Mr Biddle's word he would look after Peter,

feed him every day as he asked and allow him some time to recover his health and fitness, before being subjected to the full duties required of a stable boy.

Afore we left York, at the inn a good meal of meat, cheese, bread and ale was laid out for a starved Peter. It gave me pleasure to do this little thing for him. He was most well-mannered as he ate with much care and self-control. This impressed me greatly at the time. I would have sought an audience with the King to obtain a Royal Intervention to release Peter if all else had failed.

I watched as Sir John re-filled his pipe and lit it.

'Sir John, would you like me to make a cup of tea for you?'

'My dear Bet, have Miss Grimshaw bring up a pot of tea, and you may lay two cups at the table. There be more to say.'

Peter's Request

It be to our complete surprise when on the next day but one, after Sir John's return; Peter arrived by foot at the gates to the two fields that lead to Colesdale Hall. The walk of near five miles had been too much for him in his already weakened state. His brother Thomas found him upon the grass, laid out and totally exhausted by the effort of the walk. So, he, of course, took him in. I was there when the two of them entered the back door of the kitchen. Thomas lent a helping arm to a reluctant Peter who weakly protested there be nothing wrong with him, though we could all see this to be to the contrary. So, between us we ensured he be sat in Master Jenkins' chair, *the most comfortable*. (He didn't need to know, having tripped to the next village to source some animal feed for our pigs). Miss Grimshaw fed Peter with a large portion of her yesterday baked cheese and onion pie, which he ate with relish.

'It be no wonder you like this pie, for this be the best in the North of England without any doubt. Our cider be also of good order.' I did but add.

By now Peter was well fed with a full stomach and supplied also with a generous pot of cider. I of course later made sure Sir John knew about all this. It was his food and Peter would still be of interest to Sir John; that be a sure bet on any lottery.

Peter, who looked very much like his brother, although a good hand or more, shorter, and of much lighter build. There was an air about him which suggested he possessed a certain something more than he presented, a hidden strength perhaps? I heard as he whispered to Thomas.

'I must speak to Sir John. The matter be life and death. Can you arrange that for me Thomas? Tell Sir John that I be forever more in his debt.'

Because I was privy to this whispered exchange, I motioned

for Thomas to come over to me, which he did.

'Thomas, may I ask what the subject of the required converse with Sir John be? I would like to help if that be to your liking.'

At the time I was worried for Sir John, that he be not bothered by something trivial; though if truth be told I did expect otherwise.

I admit I had no real idea, nor any fore-warning, only my female instinct guided me, about the seriousness of the message for Sir John. For twas then when Peter came straight to me unbidden. This did catch me somewhat unawares.

'So, you be Miss Betty May I hear so much about.'

He sounded weak, as if out of breath. I could do barely anything to disassociate myself with him. In the briefest of time, I stupidly considered my safety. This be a fault of mine when directly confronted by almost any male. I could feel no other way at this time. I had but little time to speak to him before he begged me to listen to what he must pass on to Sir John.

'I do so wish you listen to me because a good man be about to mount the scaffold and hanged for no good reason. In my jail cell at York Castle, a man like my good self-did wait with me, I can only hope we be not too late. This man called Harold will admit to anyone that he attacked the cruel executioner of his brother, convicted murderer Robin Teller. Pushed beyond endurance he did give this low-begotten animal a beating, and a beating to remember, but only with his bare hands.

'Look Peter!' I replied. 'Sir John be resting at this moment in his reading room. I promise nothing except I shall put all you told me before him.'

I wasted not one moment, as I hurried up the stairs and soon found myself outside the door. . . I took a deep breath and gently rapped the door (so rare for me to do so).

'Come in,' Sir John sat relaxed with a book in one hand and his spectacles in the other. Seeing me he spoke first. 'My dear Bet, what may I do for you?'

'Oh Sir! It not be for me, and I have no wish to disturb the kind Sir.'

'Bet, come on now. You must tell me the reason which I can see so upsets you. I will of course help if I be able.'

I be not stupid, but tears came to my eyes as I related to Sir John my converse with Peter.

He understood quickly, and remarked, 'I remember Harold, chained to the wall and next to Peter. Such a sad sight if any there be.'

He thought for but a moment. 'I'll have to handle this one in a different way; Harold attacked a member of the Kings executioners, a crime which I believe must be punished by law. He looked at me. This is a person we don't know? What say you, Bet?

'I can but speak no other way, I trust Peter, he seems to me like his brother Thomas, a trustworthy soul. You must know him better than myself, and be most aware, for that they both declare their loyalty to you. Peter does wonder if you be willing under God to help another soul to receive justice. Peter struggled to walk the miles over here and says he be forever in...' Sir John, raised his hand and interrupted me.

'I'll speak to Peter, and then we'll see. My young horses need more training so a trip to York may be fortuitous in more ways than one. 'Dear Bet, will you please send the brothers up to me, here.'

I called them both over to me in the kitchen for a quiet word, much to the chagrin of Miss Grimshaw, who had entered the kitchen but a minute before.

'Sir John wishes you both to avail yourselves so he may converse with you.'

They both looked at me as if to ask what I said. I put my finger to my closed lips and they understood. 'Follow me I'll take you to him.'

I whispered to the brothers once out of Miss Grimshaw's earshot. 'Peter, I told Sir John about the circumstances surrounding your request.'

As they followed me, I did but notice how Peter had great

difficulty finding the energy to climb the steps and Thomas be forced to help him in but a small way.

I escorted the two of them and left them with Sir John. He listened and questioned them for nigh on one hour.

Then I had my call. Sir John looked tired as he spoke, 'Dear Bet, I will be away for a while. Will you run everything till I return. I mean you to keep an eye on everything that goes on. Will you do that for me?'

'Yes, Sir John of course.' I for some reason felt the burden of my small responsibility for not the first time. It be later that I realised that Master Jenkins had not been mentioned; I had made an error.

Chapter Twenty One:

Further Trouble with Master Jenkins

It was unfortunate that on this occasion Sir John had only interviewed Peter and Thomas the previous evening and I had no stomach to upset him further at the time.

In a sense, Master Jenkins sealed his own fate as regards employment at Colesdale Hall, when he took it upon himself to upset Sarah again; and so shortly after my words with him. It was on the next morn, when Sir John caught Sarah sobbing in the linen cupboard, that he got to hear all about it, before I had any chance to inform him. He asked if Sarah be unhappy and if so, what the cause of the upset be. I believe she mentioned her words with me the previous day.

So, in spite of my words to Master Jenkins, he had said some more nasty things to her, and threatened her if she gossiped to me again.

It was with considerable surprise to me when Sir John approached me on this occasion. I could see the anger in him as he came close. There could be detected a slightest of censure in his tone.

'Did you know Master Jenkins had upset Sarah?'

'Sir John, I had words with Master Jenkins only the day before your return about his words with Sarah, and suggested to him that he speak to me if he had any comment to make about her. He answered me and I felt most threatened by his countenance. I am but a young woman of slight build, and he be a bully. And I did indeed try to talk to you first, but I understood how busy you were.'

'Dear Bet, pray tell me what has happened in my absence.'

I explained how Master Jenkins had behaved towards Sarah and what I had said to him. When I described his threatening behaviour towards my person, Sir John nodded his head and spoke with an anger I have only seen once before, when he rescued me on that cold day in December all those years ago.

'There's more to this.' he said. 'He is past further warning. I want you and Sally to stay, in the family room right away until this matter be sorted out. This will not be to your disadvantage,' He added.

Somewhat at a loss what to think, I called Sarah, and we sat in unaccustomed splendour as we waited. . .

Chapter Twenty Two:

The Dismissal of Master Jenkins

March the year of our Lord 1742

Sir John be most disappointed with Master Jenkins' behaviour of late, and left with no alternative. So, on this bleak morn with this late winter's snow crisp with frost and the pond a firm field of ice, we were to see the last of him.

Good warning had been given him in the past for his behaviour, and to drink Sir John's wines and port be despicable. This warranted no reference, though Master Jenkins demanded one and, in a petty tirade, completely lost his temper. He turned nasty with Sir John, who be in danger of a threat of bodily harm. I could hear a raised voice down below in the kitchen.

I found out later that with good design, Sir John had asked Thomas to stand nearby, tall and strong, a young man who declared to me with much emotion, 'I be prepared to die, to save Sir John from any harm, nor will I tolerate any threat against him by man or beast.' Such now be his devotion to Sir John after he saved his brother from a certain hanging.

I heard that Peter offered to help Thomas but Sir John asked him to stay in the stables, in light of his weakened state. He had to agree and I witnessed his disappointed countenance at having to do so. Despite this, I heard later that Peter kept himself ready should he be needed. He was to say to me later.

'No one touches, nor insults Sir John while I breathe, so help me God!'

With no love for Master Jenkins, Thomas waited out of sight, and appeared as soon as he heard him raise his voice. With that he opened the side door to the room and stood in the doorway. He only had to show himself for Master Jenkins to stop his tirade in mid-sentence.

'This is not enough; I demand a reference. Without one I....'

His anger overcame him and his voice became low with menace. 'Sir John, if you. . .'

'If you. . . WHAT?' interrupted Thomas as he appeared by the door.

Master Jenkins looked shocked, and stared at Thomas in silence as he pondered his situation.

'I demand five guineas. Then I'll go.'

Sir John was ready, with an answer 'I said four guineas' he replied.

'No, I need five guineas,' demanded Master Jenkins.

Thomas shifted his position to be completely inside the room.

'Four pounds and ten shillings is final. You accept now. . . or you get nothing, and further more I'll report you for stealing.'

Master Jenkins made a small wince, and nodded his acceptance, 'Sir, I trust you'll see me safe to York this day?'

Meanwhile at Sir John's direction, Sarah and I sat comfortably, but in nervous expectation in Sir John's family room.

'Well Sarah,' I said. 'It be not often that we sit awaiting our work like this. Though 'tis true we face changes after all this be settled.'

'Miss Bet, I worry some, for I see changes that brought worse conditions to my friend Beatrice over in Todmorden where her new position demands more than any should.'

Unable to meet her eyes, I noticed her cheeks colour and decided to put her mind at rest.

'Sarah, you be surely safe here. I'm certain you can put your trust in Sir John and any of the other three men employed here.'

As soon as I uttered these choice words, I realised how ironic, and sad, for me to say something like this when I be afraid of every male I meet.

'I know Miss Bet. It's. . . only. . .Oh never mind!'

'Come on Sarah, let's hear it. Perchance I be able to find some remedy to whatever worries you?'

'As you are well aware, I sleep in the other attic room with

Alice sharing the space. I have no problem with her, it's just that we are in an open area with no door and it be fearsome at night under a roof that creaks so. Sometimes I worry so with sleep hard to find.'

'Sarah, I promise I'll look into your problem, which I understand well, having slept up there myself. There must be some changes because of Master Jenkins leaving us.' Her countenance brightened up as soon as I made the promise to her.'

I noticed when Sir John returned, he looked none the worst after his encounter with Master Jenkins. Sarah and I stood up in respect.

'Sarah, you can continue with your work,' he said. He closed the door behind her, strolled forward and with a flourish fully opened the red velvet curtains.

'The sun be briefly showing its face, with a beautiful rainbow. Will this be a good omen, I wonder?' he asked. As he turned to face me, the smell of wild violets reached me upon the draft from one of the partly opened windows. 'Please,' he continued, making a downward motion with his hand.

I sank into that hallowed chair opposite Sir John, the one I so favoured in the years of my service at Colesdale Hall. I still remembered to sit with a straight back as required by the

Sisters at Worsthorne Abbey, as indeed I have every time, I had the good fortune to be the guest of Sir John.

I had seen before that he had a certain poetic manner about him, though this was the first time I noticed it directed for my benefit. . .Again, I glimpsed in him something beyond Sir John the Master of Colesdale Hall. Sat down opposite me now, and enveloped by a halo of light, he looked relaxed, as he cleaned out his special pipe and re-charged it with fresh tobacco. Freshly lit, 'Ahh,' he uttered, blowing out the smoke. He puffed away for a short time while he gathered his thoughts. The smoke billowed, and a blue ray of sunbeams encircled his form. I watched with entrancement as he started his discourse with me.

'My dear Bet, we shall see no more of Master Jenkins, I have given him his leave. Such an unfortunate business this! How do you feel about it?'

'Sir, you have followed the only course open to you. Of that I be sure and a benefit to us all.'

He nodded slowly, lost in thought for a while, as he sucked away at his pipe in an effort to keep it burning. He continued. 'There will have to be some more changes,' he said, clearing his throat. 'How would you like to be head housekeeper, and take complete charge of the household?'

'If the kind Sir thinks I'm able, this be such a leap for me;

after all I be Betty May who started here as a scullery maid, but Sir, I wonder if this be more than my station in life…" Sir John interrupted again.

'Well, time has passed and you have grown, you are now nineteen years old and I have been watching you. I believe you are ready to be the Lady of the household with more responsibility. I will be pleased if you accept the position with a wage of thirty pounds per year.'

I was unable to contain myself and sat there weeping like some stupid child and I said as much.

'Oh my dear Bet, how I do hate to be the cause of a lady weeping so.'

'My kind, Sir you call me a lady, again but I be no such thing.'

'This be not some trivial title like mine Bet. You are born a lady, a true lady, as I spotted from the first days I saw you, so generous of heart, so bright and honest of nature are you.' He took another puff of his pipe, and gave up. It had gone out.

'You describe me with much kindness Sir,' I said. 'I have to tell you my mother was a kind woman who enjoyed little goodness in her life, dying at a young age, for which my heart be saddened. If only she could see me now! Alas, it be far too late for me to help her. I do believe this to be the cause of any unhappiness my countenance betrays.'

I spoke this from my heart.

'I believe your mother to be watching you now. She had a great deal of goodness in her life. She had you... If only I had known. I could have helped.'

'Sir, I believe you would have.'

Chapter Twenty Three: Sir John's Mission to York

Sir John rose to his feet at this point saying with a sigh, 'Dear Bet, as you know I have to leave this morn to see to that unfortunate man held in chains in York Jail. What I can accomplish I know not. I dislike having to leave you like this. I trust my absence will be for no longer than a few days.'

I heard later that Sir John told Master Jenkins, "We're about to leave for York. You may travel with the baggage on the rear of the coach or walk behind, the choice be yours.

Sir John told me later that Thomas agreed to drive with him out of his sight; in no comfort either, being seated on Sir John's carriage and not within. We all agreed it be worth the trouble just to get him away from Colesdale Hall.

Later, Thomas told me that Master Jenkins be fortunate indeed to be paid off by Sir John. And they left the house in time for Master Jenkins to catch the afternoon coach going to London, where his brother worked and hopefully where he was able to stay. By the time they reached York the weather matched Master Jenkins temper, violent and nasty. That be the last they saw of him.

Those few days in my new position while Sir John be away in

York, were helped by the fact that Sir John had a word with Miss Grimshaw. So, I did spend some time checking everything on the outside, and learning more about the stocking of the larder, ordering from the local grocers and a hoard of other things. Miss Grimshaw could not have been more help to me and I be most grateful to her. I endeavoured most afternoons to share a pot of tea with her. This had the result of keeping me up to date on all that went on about us, little got past her and I tried not to become reliant on her. I did believe that the dismissal of Master Jenkins be greatly to her liking, and as she said, 'There be no tears shed for him now he's gone.'

During the course of my new work, I endeavoured to do the best I could; in everything I did. There be no such work for me, as during my time as a pantry maid. I was ever mindful of this fact, and with God's help perhaps I may do some good at a future date. One day whilst I enjoyed a cup of tea with Miss Grimshaw, she did but speak personally to me.

'Bet' she said,' I must say you fill my heart with goodness, for I have seen a young girl change in but a short number of years into a confident young woman. You be made well for your future work here.'

I reached forward and patted her hand for a moment. I could see a little moisture in her eyes and knew she be speaking the truth from her heart.

All this be of great help for me as I learned as well as I be able, which made my lack of years less important. Though tis true I knew I might still need to remind myself in the future.

Before Sir John left, he asked Peter to stay at Colesfoot Hall until he came back from York. I also suspect Sir John asked him to be ready to help me, should the need arise.

As Peter grew stronger by the day, he soon came to speak with me.

'Miss Bet, I wonder if it be to your liking that I help old Henry with Goldie, the mare be young and still a little frisky. Though he works well, I believe I may have more experience with horses.'

Old Henry had been put in temporary charge of the stables. We knew he suffered badly with his back, though he would never admit to it. I knew Peter be too kind to mention why he wanted to help Old Henry.

'Peter, you speak good sense. How do you feel now, are you well?'

'Yes, better of course. I wanted to go with Sir John back to York, he wouldn't hear of it, nor would he give me work. He said I must recuperate first. Well, dear Miss Bet, here I am recuperated, and at your service,' He bowed as if to a Lady, I loved the cheeky grin on his face.

'Now Master Green me thinks you flatter me.'

'Tis my pleasure,' He lowered his head as if I be royalty, 'So I be able to help Henry then?'

'Yes of course.' My smile was broad as I realised, we had a charmer here.

'I need to be active and would like to help out. Bet if you need me at all just call me. I be forever. . .'

'Yes Peter. Thank you, I'll do that!' Now it was my turn to cut off a conversation. I dare say there be much more to learn from the kind Sir John.

At the same time as I be made head house keeper, Thomas ended up with the responsibility of being Sir John's personal valet, as well as this, he kept his post of coach driver for the time being.

Chapter Twenty Four:

Sir John's Return to Colesdale Hall

Sir John returned a few days later in the evening. Sarah came to find me in the pantry and said 'Miss Bet, Sir John wishes for your presence in the family room.'

I be going through the kitchen towels, items most necessary for the smooth, clean function of a kitchen. I considered it needful to find out how many we had. This delayed me for only minutes. My heart beat away and I didn't quite understand why. Minutes later I knocked on the door and cautiously walked in, this I believe correct etiquette now I be head housekeeper.

'Dear Bet how do I find you? Have you had a smooth ride, regarding the running of Colesdale Hall? I do so wish to know.'

'Sir John, now that you're back I feel I can work in a normal fashion, knowing that you be able to give advice should I need it.' These be words I feel to be appropriate to the occasion, 'I've had nothing I considered to be a problem.' I looked at him with expectation.

And added 'Peter has made a speedy recovery and been most helpful to Henry in the running of the stable and the exercising of the horse, and so forth.'

Sir John nodded and thought for a moment, 'Such a sorry business in York. I did eventually manage after a two day wait, to have a short meeting with the magistrate Mr J H Fisk again. This be after I heard first hand all the facts from Harold Teller about how and why he attacked the executioner. So, I put forward a plea for clemency on the grounds that Harold had been provoked, by actions beyond any reasonable behaviour. Mr Fisk be most sympathetic to my argument and confided in me that the executioner had been changed. But he be most definite that a penalty must be paid for this crime of attacking, 'The King's Executioner.'

After some debate I managed the get the execution changed to a ten-year transportation to the Australian Penal Colony in Sydney. I pointed out Harold Teller's previous good character and how he had taken charge of the compulsory archery practice as required by law. We all know why York be so good every year at this sport when the games arrive in the late Summer. Harold was a good teacher.

With this arranged, I made for Harold Teller's cell and managed to get his chains removed, in accordance with a written order of the magistrate. I had ale, bread, meat and cheese made available to him. For all this he thanked me profusely, I had to remind him that Peter Greene be the one to thank.

I must confess, I be of a good opinion regarding Harold Teller. Many a man would have done the like in a similar situation. It pleased me that at least his life was spared.

One week after Sir John's return, the grooming and general welfare of the horses were to be entrusted to a new employee. I could never say I be surprised whom this be.

'Dear Bet, Peter has just seen me and has asked if there be any work he could undertake. I thought to ask you for your thoughts on the matter,'

Seeing that Sir John did me the honour of asking me my opinion on the matter, I replied.

'I would say he be well matched to the permanent post of stable hand and handyman, for I have seen repairs he made to the stables while you were away. I feel certain that he would be honest like his brother, and always have your best interest at heart,' I spoke of the facts and his devotion to Sir John.

'Yes, well Peter told me he could not be happy at Stansfield due to the difference of opinion with the Game Keeper, and found it best to seek new employment. I formed the opinion that he wanted to work for me. So Bet, he shall be offered Thomas's old position.'

'I believe you do well with this decision, John.' I replied

Sir John smiled and nodded.

So, from that day, Peter joined us at Colesdale Hall.

Sir John had a natural hesitation before he let me learn the accounts. So extensive were they, I near lost my patience with them. I believe I had found a certain confidence, though I still worried so.

For the next few weeks, I noticed that Sir John be near to hand to show and advise. though never to interfere with me in my duties, nor to seem too close. So, after some time when I approached Sir John about these accounts, with an idea to improve them, he gave me a long look and asked if I be sure, because the accounts be most important to him. I answered in the affirmative and his answer with good humour was this.

'Go ahead Bet. Let me see what you can do, first. Then we'll see.'

The changes took only a short time to write on paper ready to show Sir John. With all this I worked to the best of my ability, *of course*. It be with not a little relief that I saw Sir John looked delighted with the workings I showed him, especially when I pointed out how savings could easily be made, now that accurate figures would be available; and all for less effort.

Chapter Twenty Five: An Unlucky Day

Friday 13th July the year of our Lord 1742

This summer day broke dull and dry, though unseasonably cold. Winter seemed impatient to show itself this year. It was not long before the fact that the date Friday the 13th be brought to my attention by Miss Grimshaw.

'Today I say prayers to the Almighty; 'Twas a Friday the thirteenth when my mother succumbed with injuries to the head, caused by a frightened horse in York, all those years ago.'

'I be so sorry to hear of this and do hope it caused you no terrible change in your circumstances.' My thoughts drifted back to my own circumstance and how alone I felt at the passing of *my* mother.

'Yes, it be a black day. It also became the day when I rose from a servant of my mother who was cook here, to being the cook for Colesdale Hall. My only wish is that she had lived a little longer.'

What could I draw from this intelligence about the thirteenth being an unlucky day when a chilled Easterly wind, though light, had blown for far too long.

It be the season when most farmers had salted their pig

carcases which they laid out to dry over hastily made wooden frames; the farmers knew what the value of a good drying wind be when preserving pork for winter food.

The day turned out to be infinitely forgettable, the curse of Friday the thirteenth. Then it happened; a disaster – the one I might have most feared. Sir John had a terrible accident while hunting deer in Gawpthorne Wood a distance of some two miles across the fields from the Hall. It was common land and available for normal hunting for the Sirs of the parish.

Sir John rode Goldie and they trotted through a rough patch of waterlogged ground, with Thomas still some way behind and out of sight. He rode forward on the trail of a buck deer and a hundred yards further on emerged from a dense, large copse of immature trees, the land now hard and ideal rabbit terrain. His horse placed a front hoof in a large rabbit hole and pitched forward with great force. This threw Sir John forward and to his right side, and unfortunately his right foot remained jammed in the stirrup.

When he heard Sir John's scream, Thomas's blood ran cold, imagining he knew not what. He was at this time only some fifty yards away and out of direct sight, so he galloped forward with no thought for his own safety and only moments later, leapt to the ground beside Sir John who lay there.

'It's my leg,' he screamed.

A quick glance at the twisted and grotesquely bent leg told Thomas that it be badly broken.

'Sir John, I have to get the help of my brother,' he said. 'I will be but ten minutes.'

Before Thomas left, he made him as comfortable as he could, and with 'all God's Speed,' jumped into the saddle and called out, 'No one will be quicker than I.'

I've heard it said that Thomas rode the distance from the woods, cross country to Colesfoot Hall, with the horse at a near gallop.

As he rode towards the Hall and before he reached our gate, he shouted out ahead 'Peter! Where be Peter? Sir John has been thrown from his horse and badly hurt! We must work our best this day,' Thomas be, almost out of breath as he entered the farm yard and dismounted.

I was in the kitchen at the time, and heard the commotion, so I ran out into the yard to hear the news.

'Where did it happen? Is he alright?' My heart felt like lead, a heavy weight inside my chest.

'Over in Gawpthorne woods, he has dire needs. We must help him. It be his leg broken. . .bbbad,' he stammered and his countenance showed the poor state of Sir John.

`How can I be of help?' I asked

He answered me not, my offer being unheard as he dashed

away.

I rushed to where I knew Peter to be working in the barn. I did but encounter him as he ran towards me, alerted by his brother's call. Once acquainted with the circumstances he started to shout orders and we all did our best to help.

'We need the cart, and a bale of hay, some sacking, some twine and two new pitch fork handles, yes, and a long piece of rope!'

Thomas recounted the rest of the sorry tale to me a short while after he returned, He told how he had led Sam. the horse, to the stable and with Peter's help unsaddled him and hitched him up to the cart in record time.

Twas then he called out to me, 'Bet, we need brandy for Sir John.,' He paused for but one moment,' and said 'Today we need help from the Lord. His broken leg be twisted and out of shape!'

Meanwhile Peter sorted through a pile of wooden planks which stood in the corner of the stables, 'This one should do,' he said and picked one as tall as himself with a good width to it and slid it onto the cart, then jumped aboard and grabbed the reins. I caught up with Thomas sat in the cart who took the bottle from me. Then with a loud 'Hayee!' Sam moved obediently forward, Peter worked the horse up to a trot, and we sped through the open stable yard gate and turned in the direction of the woods.

'With God's help we will be back shortly!' Peter shouted as he fought to control the cart. Its solid wooden wheels gave a bone jarring ride at any speed. They kept to a track which made the cart bounce from bump to bump and threatened any minute to tip over. They took the direct line to the wood, Thomas described later what happened. How they both fought in the extreme, and near frantic, to stay aboard as they crossed the landscape at top speed. Twice they had to jump off the cart to preserve life. . . had they not done so? They stopped to pick up items thrown to the ground. Thomas guarded Sir John's brandy which by some miracle or, *'Act Of God,'* stayed intact, though he earned bruises in his battle to protect it.

They arrived at the copse to find Sir John barely conscious. Peter took charge and gently grabbed his brother by the shoulders. 'Remember how I once helped Tom the master barber and that unfortunate blacksmith?'

Thomas nodded.

'This be what we do.' He proceeded to explain the steps in a low voice so only Thomas could but hear. While he listened, he found himself almost entranced by the heady scent of the yellow gorse flowers. Fore-ever-more to be remembered, nay, mixed in with the feelings of dread at what they were about to do to Sir John, as regards his broken leg.

The two brothers turned their attention to Sir John.

'Sir, I have to set your leg, and this is going to hurt,' Peter spoke to Sir John in a soft voice. 'Please Sir John, take a drink of this,' he handed him the bottle of brandy with the cork removed.

Sir John, took a swig and gagged, pulled a face and forced it down, he followed this with another and gagged again.

'Never, did I like it neat.'

'Are you ready now Sir?'

He steeled himself for a moment, and said quietly. 'Yes, go ahead!'

Using his sharp pocket knife Peter slashed the Sir's trousers from navel to ankle and exposed the broken leg. He spent some time looking at the damage to the leg, and made his decision.

'Now, Thomas, can you feel under the skin where the bone sticks out at the top of the thigh? Just here?' Sir John moaned with the pain as they gingerly examined him.

'Yes.'

'I have to pull the leg hard to stretch it, and you have to push the bones back in line. Do you think you can do that brother?'

'I'll do my best. So, help me God.' Thomas's strong words were a contrast to his feelings.

'Wait until I give the signal. I'll tell you when you have to push them into line. They should click back into place'

Peter quickly and gently looped the rope several times around Sir John's foot so as to pull on the opposite side of the leg to where the bones overlapped. Just the slightest movement elicited screams of pain.

'Be you ready Sir?

'Yes.' He answered through gritted teeth.

'Right, nod when you are ready, Thomas.' He looked at his pale faced brother.

Thomas nodded vigorously several times.

'Please forgive me Sir,' said Peter.

He steeled himself to disregard Sir John's screams which were about to start.

With one hand Peter pulled the rope, this was accompanied by an almost continuous series of screams, (these he tried desperately to ignore). With the other hand he steadied the knee as he pulled strong and hard, much force did he have to use, as he had seen that Barber Surgeon do, those six years afore.

Sir John's screams floated across that gently undulating valley. A wailing from Hell, an awful sound of torment, broken glass and ripped human bodies, squeals from the past rising through deep cracks in the ground.

Thomas knelt by the side of Sir John; his left hand ready to align the bones.

Peter spoke, 'Right Thomas, now carefully press the bones back into alignment. You'll feel them move.'

As Sir John screamed out at a higher pitch; nearby a flock of starlings rose early to the skies.

A click could be heard and Peter nodded to Thomas as he slowly relaxed the pressure on the rope. This enabled the bones to slot back together again. Peter felt sickened by the grating feel as the bones slotted together. Thomas later recalled the screams and how he also felt sick and distressed at the time.

'The screams from Sir John must have been heard throughout the forest, and far beyond,' he said to me.

Unconsciousness followed swiftly. Like a merciful cocoon it enveloped Sir John, saving him from further suffering. . . They worked quickly to wrap the leg firmly with the only clean item they had which be Peter's linen shirt. They followed this with three layers of clean new sacking packed around his leg to keep it held together, and straight, with a certain comfortable firmness. Jonathon held the new pitchfork handles in place. . . one on each side of the leg; while Peter bound the leg firmly with much twine. He checked and adjusted the binding and, with the help of Thomas, bound the other leg to the injured one.

'Now to put the board under him, we need to do it quickly while he stays unconscious.'

They rolled the Sir onto his side and placed the board next to him then rolled him back onto the board. Peter cut the long piece of rope in half and proceeded to slide a piece under each end of the board and around him. When they tied the ends together, they both had a loop of rope with which to lift up and carry him.

Now was the time to ready the cart, Peter spoke as he worked together with Thomas, 'We should spread more of the hay out like this. . . nice and thick on the cart floor, and then to make a deep bed of protection for Sir John, we must place the last piece of sacking on top of the hay.' They spread it out quickly and the thick sweet smell of the fresh mown hay filled their nostril.

'Hay mowed for the most innocent of reasons was never meant for this, though so perfectly did it serve,' said Thomas

Satisfied with the result, Peter went behind a tree and vomited.

Thomas waited for him; and soon the brothers leaned against the lip of the cart as they rested for a minute to calm down and perhaps to cool down to, despite the weather, which was anything but like summer. Thomas turned to a slightly dishevelled and shirtless Peter, 'This is a great test for us this day, and one we will be unable to forget in a hurry.'

'You are right there, this be a continuing sweat of a nightmare, and a living Hell for poor Sir John. Why would the

Lord put all this on one man, *'the kindest in England?'* Peter said.

'Peter, you are my older brother and I have always looked up to you. I'm so proud of you.'

'And I you.' He put his hand on Thomas's shoulder, 'Ready?'

'When you are!'

They had Sir John all prepared with his broken leg re-set. With only the two of them to transport Sir John back to Colesdale Hall on the cart, they were going to have to be careful not to move the affected limb.

Thomas and Peter managed with considerable effort and care, to slowly move Sir John (still barely conscious) to the nearby cart. Sam waited patiently, still hot and steamy, in the fresh mid-morn air. With good speed this well-mannered beast had pulled the loaded cart over the fields for some considerable distance.

In Gawpthorne Woods, Sir John lay lost to the world; his brown hair matted with mud. His clothes down his right side were the same.

'Thomas, when I lift will you carefully lift together with me?' Just then Sam moved his feet. 'Steady there, Sam, STEADY,' Peter spoke with just the right tone to calm him.

Despite the care the brothers took, Sir John moaned loudly at one stage as they moved him. He still appeared to be in a swoon.

'Tis with luck we are young and strong.' Thomas panted, still breathless after the lifting and positioning of Sir John onto the cart.

With that done, they rested for a moment with hands upon knees to regain their breath.

'Right . . . that's Sir John laid out upon the cart with as much comfort as we can give him. He didn't want any more brandy when I offered it to him. I can't blame him, after the way he spluttered before.' Thomas forced a grim smile.

Chapter Twenty Six: Sir John is Brought Home

It may have been Thomas's words which revived him. As Sir John awoke a strong taste caught his attention. His face, separated by a pad of straw, now be down near to the old soiled wood of a cart built before he was born. 'That brandy be strong,' was perhaps a slightly strange thing to say, it being his first utterance. There followed a kind of roar which almost reached a scream as the agony took hold again.

'Thomas, I'll lead Sam,' said Peter, if you could walk Sir John's horse back home and also steady the cart at the back? We need to keep to the path as much as we can.' He leaned against the cart and steeled himself for what had to be a slow careful journey back to Colesdale Hall.

'Yes, I'll do what I can at the back,' replied Thomas, shivering more as a reaction than because of the cold breeze. He noted that although Peter had his jacket on, he was without his shirt which he had used to bandage Sir John's leg. Peter and Thomas used all the care possible and spared not themselves; as a result, bruises were the prizes for the battles won by both brothers as they sought to steady the cart over all the rough ground. So careful they be, not to bump, nor, discomfort Sir John, for fear to disturb the newly set leg.

In the meantime, back at the Hall I caused a comfortable daybed to be made ready, in the reception room, with a pot of hot broth, and a bottle of Laudanum made ready for Sir John. I could tell we be all quietly worried, I'm sure we all hoped for the best, and tried to imagine not the worst. I heard Miss Grimshaw sniff and I supposed this be the mood of us all.

'I do but wonder what has befallen the kind Sir?' said Alice who looked worried in her ignorance.

'Sir John has broken his leg, and we put our trust in the brothers to be able to treat Sir John in a correct manner.'

I answered her thus, for I knew she missed the earlier event when Peter called for the help of Thomas. Though pushed for time, Thomas had quickly assured me that Peter be better than most in this situation due to some experience in the past. I had no time, nor reason, to ask further when Sir John lay in such worrying circumstances.

I had but little idea to what extent their expertise with broken bones might avail, my concern for Sir John's well-being be tempered by my confidence in the brothers.

Old Henry the gardener, not a person to gossip, listened to me and added, 'I believe them to be well suited for this. Peter told me about an experience while he worked as an apprentice to a smithy. He didn't go into details, but what I gathered be that he helped the local barber/surgeon in his area to set the broken arm of his master. I had to ask him about the result, be it satisfactory yay or nay. I believe he indicated his master be able to work in a normal fashion after a period of rest. This he related to me in the stables one morn while we ate our morning fare.' Old Henry rambled on sometimes; though useful in his converse on this occasion. The result be that it settled my worried heart to some degree.

Miss Grimshaw be back in her kitchen busy cooking. Both Sarah and Alice looked at a loss what to do. I instructed them, in an effort to keep melancholy out of their hearts, to help Miss Grimshaw. I guessed we would all need some sustenance after this.

Long did I wait with Henry by the gate. The cart which carried Sir John seemed to take forever. So slow a pace it had to take. Eventually they arrived back safely with Sir John laid out and groaning with every unavoidable movement. Peter organised us to carry Sir John on a wool blanket. The carrying of the kind Sir tugged at my heart as he moaned in agony at every movement. Only minutes later, and after some struggle, with Peter and Thomas taking most of the weight, we carried Sir John into the house to a small reception room on the ground floor. Much care was taken, as he was lowered by our willing hands onto a comfortable small bed we had prepared; a warm log fire aglow nearby and warm woollen blankets were there to aid in the comfort of Sir John. It was here that the brothers removed the board and the bonds which fastened his legs together. The result was to settle him down and allow some degree of pain reduction.

'I be pained to put you all to this trouble on my account. Oh, so careless of me!'

I could hear the relief in Sir John's voice to be home. Then he drifted into a swoon; of which he had no recollection later.

For the first time I felt the full weight of office as head of the household. Thomas spoke to me so only I could hear, 'Bet, you can count on Peter and myself to help you with your duties.'

'Thank you, Thomas,' His kind words touched me and gave me a feeling of confidence and ability to undertake anything I desired. I knew my limits but it was leastwise a comfortable feeling.

My first thought be to cause the doctor to be called. When I mentioned this, Peter who looked drained, suddenly jumped into life and did insist he be the one to call him.

Less than an hour later Peter returned with the doctor in due haste on horseback as one would expect, if you consider who the patient be. I first explained the circumstances and escorted the doctor to the room where Sir John reposed. After he spent some time with him, the doctor gave me instructions to keep the leg bandaged with the splint in place and make sure he stayed on his back, for at least the next two weeks. He left with promises to return in two days.

Later that day I had Miss Grimshaw make a pot of tea and invited an upset Peter and Thomas to join us. This was long after Sir John had settled down and be left to sleep in comfort. Peter told us (though to be honest he addressed me mostly) of the urgent need in Gawpthorne Woods to set Sir John's leg. At this stage he became upset as he addressed me so.

'Oh, Bet you can't imagine the pain I had to inflict upon Sir John who so recently saved my life. He screamed out so; and the brandy had but small effect.' He shook his head and his voice faltered, 'I swear I felt his pain, the kind Sir; he be the last person. . .' He choked back a sort of cough.

I reached over to him and placed my hand upon his shoulder. I felt him quiver.

'It be alright, we understand!' I said looking him in the eye.

'You and Thomas truly did a great service to Sir John,' said Miss Grimshaw, nodding as she spoke.

'Yes, I agree, Miss Grimshaw be right. I be sure of that!'

Thomas explained, 'His leg had to be correctly reset, otherwise Sir John would never have been the same again. A cripple without any doubt.'

I remember Miss Grimshaw stood up and said, 'There's a large black treacle cake in the pantry that I wager you'll both like.'

It was at this time I noticed that Peter wore his best shirt, the one he kept for Sundays in church. I mentioned it to him and he just shrugged and said but little.

I noticed Sir John had linen wrapped as a first layer around his leg. That was when I guessed that Peter be the owner of the wrapping around Sir John's leg. So, I asked Thomas to enlighten me and he did mention that, "Peter did use his linen day shirt for the first wrapping around Sir John's leg."

When I heard this, I knew what I had to. I excused myself, 'I'll be but a minute.'

I knew there be more important matters, not the least the Sir's well-being which be on every one's mind. Nevertheless, I made straight for Sir John, who by good fortune be partly rested and quiet, but more importantly awake.

Unsure of exactly what to say I did blurt out, 'Sir John, I'm sorry to trouble you at a time like this, but Peter had to use his shirt to cover your leg and now has none but his Sunday shirt to wear. Sir John answered me thus, 'Dear Bet, go into my wardrobe and select the one most suitable and give it with my blessings. Without those two, I just don't know...'

When given the shirt, Peter jumped to his feet and to my surprise kissed me on my cheek, and spoke, 'Bet you are the very best. I never for one moment expected this.'

I fear I did blush on this occasion.

So that was how we ended that Friday the thirteenth. Very little of that large sweet cake was left on the plate by the time we retired to bed.

Had the matter been known; I learned later that a wave of farmers and hired hands would have insisted on helping to transport Sir John back to Colesdale Hall. The number of visitors and well-wishers testified to the regard felt by our neighbours. There was much good Yorkshire ham given to Sir John on these visits from which we all benefited.

At first Sir John be most poorly, and in terrible pain. He seldom ate his food. Aware of what be expected from me, I put on a brave face. I hoped to cope to the master's satisfaction with the circumstances. To this end, I organised Miss Grimshaw to have his favourite food cooked for him. For my own needs I cared not, and it would be true to say I ate little more than Sir John.

On the fourth morn I took breakfast to a deathly pale Sir John, and tried yet again to feed him a little porridge. He shook his head. I could not stop myself and I said to him, 'Sir, I implore you! You must eat to keep your strength up.' I must have shown my concern for he turned his head to look up at me.

'You really care, don't you Bet?'

'We all want you to recover Sir.'

'Alright Bet, I'll take some porridge, I have but little appetite.'

Several days later I felt in much finer spirits now that an improved Sir John said to me.

'Do you know, Bet, the doctor be very pleased by the way my leg has been set? He said that he couldn't have done it better himself. I'm so grateful to everyone, for what has been done and the way you are all looking after me.'

I still experienced some difficulty and had my hands full as I tried to keep him in bed, for he always wanted to be active. I took it upon myself and cared for him as if I be his mother. So much do I feel I owe Sir John.

Thomas and Peter showed themselves to Sir John constantly so as to be able to help in his care, and help me whenever needed. They were of great help when he had to move as be natural. To give him a welcome surprise they placed a coat of paint over the stables and other out buildings, all in much need of this treatment; and enhanced the effect by a general tidy up around the yard. This could be seen from the side window on the second floor where Sir John now rested. If truth be known I was not aware of this work until I heard Sir John exclaim. . .

'Well. . . 'pon my soul! What do I spy but a yard full of new looking buildings?' Sir John's face beamed, 'I'll wager that be the work of Peter and Thomas. I've noticed the horses get plenty of exercise as is proper. I feel that I owe them much. My Dear Bet what say you?'

'Sir, I believe you be most fortunate to have the employ of these two brothers who I believe will continue to do you proud in the future.'

The coach be the next interest of this handy pair; which they cleaned and polished until it be transformed into a fine machine. This were to the surprise and delight of Sir John, who be lost for words when he eventually caught sight of it.

As he improved, Sir John took an interest in me and seemed to enjoy our general discourse when my work permitted. He seemed to relish our daily discussion about the next day's menu, and other things that were not about my work. I noticed the way he looked at me; which made my heart beat so. But soon he complained to me.

'I have so much paper work to see to, I fear I shall never be rid. A new pair of curtains is required for the family room, I must see to it and the carpet in the library, it is getting worn. Bet. There be so much I must see to.'

'Sir, if I may be so bold as to give an opinion, it would please me so and be to your benefit, if you were to rest and try not to move and leave myself, with the good and willing help of Thomas and Peter to keep the house running.' Not long ago I would not say anything so forward as this.

Sir John looked at ease as he sighed, 'My dear Bet, how nice it be of you to put my mind at rest.'

'Sir John, you have helped me in more ways than one. I'm forever in your debt.'

'When we're alone, you can call me 'John' from now on.'

A smile appeared on my face. This I couldn't erase, nor would want to; so wonderful did I feel.

'Dear Bet, I feel a warm glow about you, which I'm sure this will champion my recovery, you light up the room and my heart. Yes, my heart.'

I looked at his eyes, and did glimpse into those bright brown windows at a kind loving soul. They gazed and sparkled so for me I know not how long I gazed back. My own blue eyes must have been wide open for him to see my nerves and senses heightened. The sun beams had never before shone so bright through the window.

Oh, those flowers! 'What thoughts did invade my senses. I be acutely aware of the sweet powerful scent of a vase close by; overwhelmed, the sensation loaded over me; I had but no time to wonder, because it all crashed down, when I heard.

'Excuse me, Mistress Bet can I have the key to the linen cupboard?'

My thoughts were cruelly invaded by these few words. It took a little while to sink into my mind; a mind full of wonderful new feelings. Almost ready be she to ask again, before I replied as if in a dream "Right Sally I'm coming,' A little unhappy be I at that interruption, a cruel hand dragging me back from some higher place; back down to a cold reality. I felt so guilty; yet indeed, how I did wish to return.

'Sarah please, 'I said. 'When I be in the presence of Sir John, only call me for something important, or an emergency.' I detected a slight smile upon her face. I wondered what she noticed upon mine?

Later, Peter and Thomas, helped me by moving certain furniture so as to be able to remove the large carpet out of the library. With great effort we dragged it outside to hang over a washing line, where between us we spent hours as we laboured to beat the dust out of it. When we replaced it, we turned it around so the wear be out of sight and hidden from view. As regards the red velvet curtains in the family room, I believed they only needed but a clean. Miss Grimshaw noticed the effort we did put into the beating of the carpet.

'Sir John will be most surprised when he sees the carpet you've cleaned.'

'Now for the curtains in the family room. They are going to be a problem; they are so long.' I did but mention.

'Not at all, I know Mr Armstrong in the village. He is the local fuller and I'm sure he can clean them for you. If you like, I can go now and ask him to come and take a look.'

He arrived in the afternoon, a most helpful man. 'I be 'appy to take them down an' clean them lovely red velvet curtains, an' 'ang them back in place. It be my pleasure Mam,' he said as he doffed his hat to me.

He returned them a week later and they looked like new. This pleased me no end, I felt sure the Sir would be pleased also, when he eventually got to see them, and all done for the reasonable sum of four shillings and nine pence.

Chapter Twenty Seven: Sir John Became Impatient

Tis but only ten days after the accident when Sir John called for me. At the time I be with Sarah as we prepared his bedchamber. I knew well that Sir John be bored and determined to stand up and walk today. For this reason, I quickly sent Sarah on an errand and explained to her why.

I could but see the determination in his countenance when I approached him; so, I held my tongue. I understood how he felt with the sun out today and most beautiful outside.

His request for my help to enable him to stand, I felt duty bound to refuse. When he asked for Sarah to help us, I be pleased I had sent her on some small errand. So, I had no need to evade the request, for it be beyond me to lie to Sir John.

'John, if this be your wish then I'll summon Peter and Thomas to help.'

'Yes, my dear Bet I'll wait.'

I didn't trust him to remain seated with his leg stretched out, and I fear I gave him a certain look. This I had no authority to do and I felt I may have gone a little too far, when I realised, he read my look.

'I'll remain so, have no fear,' he said.

Twas my hope that any guilt I felt be hidden, for my reason

for calling for the brothers in my mind be a little cowardly, (though of some sense of a common nature, which may be brought more effectively to Sir John; than I ever could).

Soon I had the pair of them by Sir John; each holding an arm to help him to his feet. He managed to stand with a slight difficulty, but proved unable to hold his own weight; he tried to take a step and sat down again.

'We'll remove the splints now,' commanded Sir John.

'Sir, it is far too soon!' Peter warned in an anxious voice.

'No, it'll be alright.' said Sir John.

'Sir if you remove them now; I will have to find other employment immediately. I cannot face the consequences of seeing you as a cripple.' Peter's head was lowered as he spoke.

'You really mean it don't you?' Sir John looked incredulously at him.

'I be unable to watch yourself, or anyone else harm you Sir, I would have to leave. Sir if I may suggest, perhaps we can come every day and allow you to stand and move about? You need at least three weeks in splints; you have a bad break there; I have experience in this matter,' continued Peter.

'And what do *you* think Bet?'

'Sir, I think you know the answer to that question. Peter speaks with good sense. What say you, Thomas?' I looked at him.

'What Peter says will be correct. He has more experience in these matters than I. I say the longer the better; give the bones a chance to heal.

'Alright! This will be done as you suggest, Peter.'

After they left, a quietness descended into the family room. A small matter demanded my attention and I returned to see Sir John who be sat up with his back to me on his daybed, leant forward with shoulders a quiver as he made a small sound, it be a few moments before I realised that he sobbed so.

'Oh, my dear Bet, I am so touched, why be everyone so kind to me?' He spoke with a soft broken voice.

I've never heard him in such low spirits before, I swear I knew not why he should be so and I spoke from my heart.

'I'll tell you John, it's because they love you, as we all do. . . *AS I DO.*" I said it without thinking, for how could I think? For I had only just realised it myself. Now I knew.

At this time, I am by his daybed, so I perch on the edge. He placed an arm around me and leaned forward, he put his head on my shoulder and kissed me on the cheek. 'Oh, my dear, dear Bet. . . I do so feel the same for you and I wish you to know this,' he said.

I turned my head towards him; we look at one another again,

and before I knew it, we kissed. I'm carried to new heights that both scare and entice me. After an eternity, we stopped and he placed his head on my shoulder. My old fears are gone for the moment.

'My Bet, you have given me new life.'

Chapter Twenty Eight:

Sir John's Convalescence

Tuesday 7th August the year of our Lord 1742.

A pale, gaunt looking Sir John sat relaxed with his leg stretched out on the chaise-longue. The wooden spade handle splints that Peter and Thomas had affixed to his leg, some three weeks ago, were still in place. I knew Sir John wanted them removed at the first opportunity. I also knew this to be far too early, the doctor told me in confidence that it be better to keep them on longer rather than shorter.

Today I organised Miss Grimshaw to work upon Sir John as he convalesced in the sitting position in his drawing room.

'Miss Grimshaw, can you get your special scissors out and see to Sir John's hair, please. I believe he needs a trim.'

I knew they to be sharp because she trimmed my fringe yesterday.

'Will that be right away, Mam?'

'Finish what you're doing first.'

'I'll do it now if that suits your good self. There be nothing urgent in here at this moment.'

'Then right away it is. Give me two minutes to prepare Sir

John. You know what he is like with his hair.' I couldn't help the slight smile which crossed my face.

Sir John was in good need of her services, so I had made a comment to him about not letting it get too long. When he agreed I took that as a request. In my mind a man of his class should always look his best.

'Alright Bet, go ahead. Get Miss Grimshaw up here with her scissors.'

For some short time, she clipped away at his hair, then he did the unthinkable. Without thinking, he lit up his pipe with a flaming sulphur match.

I noticed her grimace and cough as she proceeded to work in double quick time to finish the trimming of his brown hair. Her scissors worked at a pace and formed a kind of blur. Soon results showed as a sharp cut throat blade used with surprising skill and dexterity did its work. This was the quietest I had heard her work, no longer did her chatter fill the room. I did only hear her occasional cough which went unheeded by Sir John.

At this stage it was beyond my station to mention the subject of the pipe to Sir John.

Poor Miss Grimshaw! I knew she had no liking for Sir John's tobacco smoke. Her speed belied her well fed and adequately covered body, so typical of a cook. Soon she satisfied herself of the result and turned to him.

'Would that be all the good Sir requires?'

Sir John had a quick look in the hand glass which she held for him. He nodded, 'Much neater now!' He declared.

She managed a thin smile and wasted little time as she bid her leave of him, 'I'll tend to the kitchen now if that be all.'

'Thank you, Miss Grimshaw. I'll get Alice to sweep up,'

Her retreat from the room seemed a little hasty, and I noticed she wafted a hand across her face as she headed for the stairs.

I was well aware I had enough problems on my plate as I walked round to have a good look at Sir John. I had to admit he did look tidy now, like a true Sir in his red silk smoking jacket. I know not if there be anything strange about me for, I have to admit to a liking for the strong smell of his expensive tobacco.

Alice curtseyed to Sir John and swept up the room. Soon we were on our own again. With this he visibly relaxed and gingerly shifted his position slightly for comfort, I noticed he gritted his teeth.

'John, do you still feel discomfort in your leg.'

His expression changed. 'Not at all Bet.'

I looked at him with a raised eyebrow, and he noticed.

'Well, I can't lie, there be a little unease over the top of my leg. And it does itch so on the occasion.'

'The doctor did say,' "this would be natural after such a bad break," I liked not what I suspected to dwell upon his mind and hoped to be wrong in my suspicion. My only concern was for Sir John's recovery.

Sure, enough a little later it be on the same afternoon when my fears were proved just; I had to be stern with him again when I caught him trying to put on his riding boots.

'John, pray may I ask, what do you think you are doing?'

It felt normal for me to converse in such a fashion on these days, with a direct address which he has encouraged from me. He stopped and looked at me almost like a naughty boy, then gave me a smile.

'My dear Bet. How the lady blooms; and I find tis so wonderful to see. Please help me remove this boot I know it will be but another week yet before I can wear them.'

'Yes John, it will be a week or more.' I did flash my bright blue eyes from below my neat newly cut brown fringe. My effort was not wasted, for he did look at me in the way I desired. I helped to remove the boot and he sat back on the settee.

'Please join me,' he said, as he patted the seat with his hand.

This I did and sat not too close to him but he moved closer to me and put his arm around me.

'I now look forward to the future, how about you Bet?'

'I too, but John I will be a mistress to no one. Please

understand why I say this thing, I do truly love and respect you. My mother, may God bless, made me promise not to not end up like her,' I hesitated for a moment, 'Oh my goodness what is to become of me?' I asked. I uttered this but low in a soft and feeble voice. My mind was everywhere, I worried so.

'My dear, dear Bet, my intentions are honourable as you shall see.'

With that he leapt forward and kissed my cheek, to no great resistance from me. 'I want to give you something, what would you like Bet?'

'Just get better John, that's all I ask.'

'Those curtains look like new and the library carpet is bright and clean. Dear Bet, you never cease to amaze me.'

Chapter Twenty Nine:

I Learn About Sir John's Earlier Life

Sir John's convalescence continued under our care. Unable to stand for long at first, only after weeks of steady assistance from Peter, and Thomas, was he able to walk a little on his own without pain, this within nearly two months after the accident.

Sir John and I had much time for discourse during his convalescence, and he eventually told me about his childhood on the family sugar plantation in Jamaica. He spoke of the private tutors and coloured nannies, and how he was a spoiled and naughty child with a privileged life.

At the age of just eight years, he lost his mother and older brother who were returning from a trip to England, on a ship that sank in a storm. This shock, a terrible introduction to mortality for a child; changed him from this happy carefree little boy to a naughty child. His father never got over the loss of his wife and eldest son. John also missed his older sister, Emily, who was sent to a private school in England.

Sir John married at the age of sixteen years in Jamaica, the couple lived in their own house on the plantation with his father. Tragedy was never far behind John; when his father died suddenly a few months after the wedding; this left John to grow up quickly. He had to take charge of this large family business at a young age and being only partly prepared for this onerous task, with much responsibility; he harboured a life-long dislike for the slave system, and found he could never be truly happy with such oppression of mankind.

Nevertheless, he battled on for nearly ten years until another tragedy befell him. His wife died. He took this opportunity to change his life, and to leave the painful memories behind; he sold everything in Jamaica and only retained certain family interests in London. He decided to move to Colesdale Hall in Yorkshire, the family home he had seen only once before.

Chapter Thirty: The Visitors

Mid November the year of our Lord 1742.

It was now some four months after his accident and Sir John had fully recovered, although he felt the need for a stick. I swear it be to please me, when he declared, he would go hunting on horseback no more. This by all things in God's will I could hardly believe, that he should consider me so.

Sir John left me in charge for a few days, when he departed for a trip to London. By this time, I had confidence in myself which was bolstered by Sir John, who praised me for my small efforts. Now I felt able to comfortably carry that responsibility.

He told me, 'My dear Bet, due to my accident I am well behind with my investments and in urgent need to visit my bankers in London. I also have an important meeting as an Insurance Underwriter which I must shortly attend. And of course, there be other urgent matters requiring of my attention.'

'All will be well here in Colesdale while you be away, now Master Jenkins be gone.' I assured him.

Little was there to report in the first days of Sir John's absence, except for our first litter of pigs born to Snowdrop. Peter had built a proper pigsty for her with a roof like a large dog kennel and a small enclosure. She repaid our kindly attention which worked to our advantage, for soon we had twelve dear little squealing piglets. This idea to rear pigs was an idea I put before Sir John not long ago. This did cause extra work for Peter and Thomas who apparently had to help poor Snowdrop who, being tame, minded not the attention. She started that night at about ten of the clock and ended at six of the clock in the following morning. They were both worn out and I excused them both for a few hours during the day.

On the third day of Sir John's absence, we received a knock on the door. When I opened it, I found before me this lady; who appeared overdressed even for church, and spoke in one of those false, superior London accents.

'Pray bring Sir John to the door, child.'

This did cause me to gaze at her in some confusion. Perchance my ears deceived me? But with her countenance unchanged, it was with some difficulty I held my tongue. After a short pause I answered.

'Sir John is away at the moment.'

I was unable to stop myself, and I stared at her. I knew full well I shouldn't, but I couldn't help myself. Perched upon her full head of red hair, was a tiny bonnet of dark green fabric the strangest I had ever seen and tied securely under her chin with a pink silk ribbon. Far too small, it moved with every word she spoke and looked ridiculous.

'Sir John knows me well. I shall bring my two lovely and well-educated daughters with me on Saturday, at two thirty sharp. I trust he will be here?' This she said more as a command than a question, as she regarded me closely.

'Um. . .Yes, Sir John should be here at that time. Who shall I say called?'

'Why it's Mrs Slaughter of course,' She replied as if the words had been stupidly asked.

She looked me up and down, taking her time with terrible manners. 'And who may I ask are you?'

'I be the Head Housekeeper, madam."

'And your name?'

'Mistress May of course,' Oh my wicked tongue!

Without further ado she charged off in the direction that she had come, accompanied by a short, 'Huh!'

Sir John returned that Friday evening full of life after his visit. So, I passed on the message.

'John, there is a Mrs Slaughter coming to visit you tomorrow, at two thirty, with her two daughters.'

'A Mrs Slaughter you said. . . with two daughters?'

Sir John was lost in thought for a moment. Then I noticed the colour drain from his face.

'Oh no! Not *THAT Mrs* Slaughter!'

'I'm afraid so,' I said with a smile.

'It be a good five years since I last saw them. Will you serve afternoon tea when they come? I would like you to observe what happens.' He looked a little lost in thought.

'Of course, I'll check what we have in the kitchen.'

His attitude did cause me to wonder what this be about.

Saturday arrived and it soon became time to receive the visitors. On the half hour, the clock chimed as if to signal the door bell, which promptly rang. I answered the door, and in that same blue cloak and voluminous red silk over dress, with that hat still perched there, she stood before me. I had a silly thought that she had left it on her head all that time. I took a deep breath and waved her inside.

As she advanced to the doorway, she held a hand of each of her two daughters and raised them in a valiant attempt to look regal. This effort unfortunately had the opposite effect and looked plain ridiculous; I believe this was for the benefit of Sir John who fortunately never answered the door. This she should have known. I hid my smile.

I escorted the guests through the house to the formal room. Guests they were by name only; you could have been excused for thinking they had come to buy the house.

This gave me the opportunity to observe closely the twin girls who were both perfect copies of their mother. Mrs Slaughter stopped with her daughters at the various rooms, and as we passed she opened three doors completely uninvited, as she kept up her commentary.

'To your left, is a good-sized room that would make an ideal day nursery. To the right, I would have that room as the lounge, redecorated of course. We don't need all these overpaid servants, idle, the lot of them,' said loud so I could hear.

Sir John was waiting for them inside the formal room with his hands behind his back so as not show any discomfort if it be so.

'Please sit and make yourself comfortable,' he said as I led them in.

'Such manners, such breeding, listen girls did you hear that? Said Mrs Slaughter in her obviously put on fake voice.

'Yes, Mama.'

'Yes, Mama.'

This was said in rapid succession, by the two deeply freckled young red haired girls.

'And to what do I owe the honour of this visit may I ask?' Sir John asked, facing Mrs Slaughter.

"I've come with my two daughters, Felicity and Candice, to visit you on a social basis,' said the mother.

'You can see how well reared they are, totally unspoilt. Aren't you girls?' she asked proudly.

They both answered at once, 'We are. We are.'

Sir John told me that at this stage he felt he must make no comment about the young ladies to Mrs Slaughter, lest, 'Lord Help Him,' she believed he be interested in them.

'Would you all like tea.' Sir John was much relieved to change the subject.

'Yes, but we only drink Lapsang,' commanded Mrs Slaughter.

I left the room; I had already gained an idea why they were here.

Some few minutes later, as I laid out the teapot, china and a cake on a small table, my idea was confirmed when I heard the word 'dowry 'mentioned by her.

Stood to one side, I had time to have good observance of the two young ladies, and formed the opinion that they had the undoubted benefit of an easy life. This was attested by the more than generous covering of flesh over their heavy bones. They applied themselves with silence and diligence to the task of removing the burden from the plate of a rather large fruit cake. With ribbons in their hair, like young girls, I would say they were about twenty years of age.

Sir John nodded to me and I left the room without regret.

The tea was consumed to the never ceasing chatter of Mrs Slaughter, and the stone like silence from the twins, who both sat there in obvious discomfort. Eventually it was time to leave and she fired a parting broadside.

'I'll be hearing from you shortly then? Don't take too long as my girls are most popular, and I have a full appointment book.'

'If I have any thoughts on the subject I'll be in touch,' said Sir John as he shut the front door with a sigh of relief.

He turned back and returned to the room as I cleared up.

'Do you know, dear Bet, what all that was about?'

'Yes John, I think I have but a fair idea,'

'It's the cattle market,' he said with a chuckle.

'Really, that's not polite,' I said, unable not to smile at the thought.

'With two fine porkies for breeding,' he said. Unable to restrain himself any longer, he collapsed onto the settee in a fit of laughter, tears rolling from his brown eyes.

At first, I kept a straight face, and then had to join him in laughter.

Before I knew it, he kissed me passionately, and it was with some slight difficulty that I might keep control of the situation, for by now I was beginning to understand why I felt fearful. It was nothing to do with Sir John.

'I have something for you Bet,' he said, as he reached into his pocket. His hand reappeared and he clutched a small dark blue velvet box. This he handed to me and my surprise was complete, for when I opened it there displayed before me, shone a silver ring. It be set with a large clear stone with a beautiful sparkle, surrounded by small red stones. I later proved myself right that the stones were rubies which did encircle a large diamond.

'Dear Bet, please accept this as a gesture of friendship between us.'

My left hand trembled so as I slid the ring onto my middle finger of my right hand, a perfect fit. I could not hide my delight. Without thought I threw myself at Sir John. He had no time to react to the kiss on the cheek, for I rushed to the window, like an excited child.

'Oh John. . .' I moved the ring this way and that way in the light, 'never in my life have I seen such beauty, nor could dream of owning anything so. . . for once, I was at a loss to find the words, and jumped back into his waiting arms. He caught me and laughingly said.

'Steady there.' This time I couldn't escape, and with his arms around me we kissed.

Chapter Thirty One:

The ring box and Miss Grimshaw

Mid June the year of our Lord 1744.

If perchance anyone should have read this far, of my poor life, then I believe they may find some small interest in my continued story. This be of a natural ambition to be respectable and comfortable. I had no wish to return to the poverty of my early childhood. I told it with honesty and my hope be of modesty also, that this would be the judgment passed over me by my betters.

I can recall how on that momentous day those two years ago, when Miss Grimshaw noticed the ring box which showed through my pocket; this was before I had made up my mind whether to mention it or not. This did put me out of my own comfort and surprised me no small amount.

It was just after Sir John gave me the friendship ring. I left him with work on my mind. Sarah was almost finished on the second floor, with only the two fires to tend to, and the wipe down of the marble surrounds. As I walked to the stairs over newly polished boards, I felt so happy with my life. Nay I be more than just happy. I did feel almost giddy. Could I be dreaming this? A twinge of disappointment struck me as I questioned myself, 'Did I truly deserve my good fortune.' There goes that dark part of me again. So, my mind was everywhere except on what I be doing. I descended the brown stone stairs down to the kitchen to make my regular daily check to ensure sufficient food be in the larder. Tis true I be not concentrating as I should.

Twas on the fourth step from the kitchen floor when I stumbled, 'Oh my, whoops,' I called out when my left ankle twisted as my right foot shot out past the step.

'Bet!' Miss Grimshaw called out. She was only but a yard away and stood at the table. She dived forward, grabbed a handful of my pinafore and softened my arrival on the floor. At this stage of my life, I be taller, but was still like a scarecrow, and weighed but little.

Luckily, I managed to grab the stairs banister with one hand and arm. This saved my bones. Though my foot be now sprained and most painful.

'Ow! I can't. . .I can't stand now. How can I do my work?' I worried before I needed to.

'It's first things first. Let me bring a kitchen chair for you and we'll get you seated and comfortable now.'

A sharp pain stabbed my ankle every time I tried to stand on it.

'How stupid of me. To twist my ankle so.' I be totally at fault because of my self-indulgent feelings after my meeting with Sir John.

'Miss Bet, put your weight on the good foot, while I help you to this chair.'

Soon I found myself sat at the table as be normal at this time of day. Meanwhile Peter was called to tie a tight bandage around my foot.

With the blessing of Sir John, we enjoyed a cup of tea every afternoon. This was unthinkable not long ago. So, when I asked him about the matter, he looked at me and said, "My dear Bet, I wish you to make such decisions.' He had a most kind expression as he looked at me.

I answered in the only way I knew I must, 'John, tea is expensive and I only want you to know that I asked. And for you to know it be under my supervision at all times.'

Sir John leaned forward and squeezed my hand. His touch did something to me. My heart beat so fast inside my chest, and I fear my cheeks burned so and needed no rouge for beauty's sake. Though I confess to no use of this face powder.

'Bet, I have confidence in your judgment.'

Though now of an adult age I still be guilty of an occasional day dream as I relaxed with my cup of tea.

I experienced a slight shock as I sat at the table, when Miss Grimshaw asked of me.

'Bet forgive me, but what is that ring box doing in your petticoat pocket that I cannot fail to observe?'

'You have got me there, Miss Grimshaw. What do you want me to tell you? I tell no lies as you know. But must I tell you everything?' I looked at her.

Just as I conversed with her. Sarah walked down into the kitchen.

'Be there a cup for me?' she asked in a somewhat cheeky way. I felt pleased that she spoke so, though most unlike her.

'Yes of course. Please, sit with us,' I said, indicating a place next to me.

Miss Grimshaw's eyes never left me as she poured out all our teas. We understood why she simmered so.

At this time, I had a prick of conscience,Alice!' I called out loud so she could hear me in the scullery.'

I heard the strained voice of a young girl (whom I knew well). 'Yes, Miss Bet.'

'You must join us for a cup of tea.'

'Oh yes, thank you Miss Bet.'

Alice had taken my place as pantry maid, and I had no wish that she continued the same way as had been the case with me. So, almost from the beginning she dined with the rest of the staff at the kitchen table. 'You may as well,' I said 'because pantry maid be a position in name only. Now you to be at the table with equal rights to everyone else.'

Miss Grimshaw chipped in, as I expected, 'I thought an afternoon tea be for only the betters in our class?'

'In this house there be no betters, and, no class. There be a leader and it be me, under Sir John of course and that be all.'

'So, what be in your petticoat pocket then?' Nosiness infected her enquiry.

I liked that not, so I answered her in like manner, 'When I want you to know I will tell you. I don't wish to offend you, but I'll take the risk. Until then I suggest you mind your own business. It be as simple as that.'

Bless her, nosy to the end. She answered me, as if unable to do otherwise. 'But you have something in your pocket. You must tell me what this may be!'

I gave her that by now weary look. 'We're starting that again, are we?'

'Err, what, starting what?'

'Being ignorant. In other words, ignoring what I say.' I stared at her. She opened her mouth like a fish from the village pond, looked at me, and wisely shut it again.

You may well wonder why I write in this way. You see this be a time when I learned how to use my position to control my responsibilities. This turned out to be a wise converse between myself and Miss Grimshaw. I noticed in future dealings with her a kind of hesitation in her converse with me. I believe this be due to her biting her tongue to avoid me using mine.

The tea was another matter. Not as expensive in those days as it used to be, it was originally regarded as a luxury item and kept under lock and key.

The last time she mentioned the matter I did ask of her, 'How much does an extra cup of boiling water in the pot cost Sir John?' Miss Grimshaw said no more about the subject.

Chapter Thirty Two: Memories of Yesterday

All this took place some two years ago. As I sat there on the side of my bed with my new gold nibbed pen (from Sir John) in my hand and ready to write as I felt, I found as I still stared wide eyed into the looking glass on the wall over the dressing table, my expression would be of disbelief to anyone privy to my private moments (this be my fault of disbelief). Does the glass see the same image as me, of my long shiny, brown hair brushed back twice a day with my neat fringe which frames my bright blue eyes? How could I possibly have been such a short time ago, a waif, a child born out of wedlock, and now be this normal young woman which stared back at me, with a twenty-one-year-old body? Could I truly be here and hold the position of Head Housekeeper? Surely not, this must be a cruel dream? I fear that I weep a little for the truth (which methinks I know). For what does the glass see? Does it see me still as the waif, a non-person of no worth before the law, bigger but still worthless? I do but wonder will I ever leave these feelings behind me? I still fear I shall awake as if from a dream in most distressed and disappointed circumstances, as would be appropriate for a bastard before God in my time. After all these years I do still doubt myself on the occasion.

I pinch an arm for reassurance, but I'm not reassured. For what peace of mind before God, can this bring? Do you not pinch yourself in dreams? I pinch again, and feel something on my hand; this brings on a flood of emotion, YES, but why would a poor wretch such as I, have this object of a lady's desire?

Part of my senses return. And I can still hear Sir John's words those two years ago and how they echoed in my ears. I allowed myself the self-indulgence of a little tear of relief, for I should be so fortunate. After a good laugh with Sir John, a surprise awaited me. He turned towards me and at the same time his hand disappeared into a pocket of his brown corduroy under jacket.

'I have something for you Bet.'

I remembered his words which still flowed through my mind. . . 'yesterday's memories,' which I treasure more than gold, for how much happiness could a young woman from my background have in one lifetime? My blessings be now far too numerous to count. . .

So tis with considerable relief I thank God, and do shake off these images in my mind as I must recall that there be much for me to thank providence and if truth be known Sir John for.

A knock on my bedroom door shocked me out of my reverie. Sarah had a message for me. 'Mistress Bet, the dressmaker has arrived, and is downstairs awaiting you.'

'I'll be but one minute.' Quickly I gather my wits and realised that I should be ashamed of myself for 'tis early noon. I daydreamed on the Sir's paid time; how bad did I feel. The sheets for washing lay in a pile at my feet, and the excuse for me to be by my bed at such a time.

In my defence if there were to be any, Sir John had left me wondering now for two years. I felt a build-up of excitement, because I came to understand that he would never dis-service me and a certain second sense (perhaps because I be a woman) told me that this be the way he wanted our friendship to grow. I know of no other claim for his affection and certainly not Mrs. Bradshaw's 'two daughters,' may the Lord forgive me for the thought. I smiled as I recalled no other communication from her had been forthcoming.

I had yet to find out why he insisted on paying for a new travel dress and coat for me. How could I feel anything but contentment in my destiny as God had chosen? I knew I should not question his reasons, and 'twas to my discredit if I did so. He had bought me 'travelling clothes.' 'So, he wants me to travel,' This was fine, I told myself but the source of much worry, bad dreams and imagined reasons. I did accept I be prone to worry, I felt this to be again the result of my childhood experiences.

Sir John was away at this time on another trip to London to see his bankers with a promise that he would tell me more upon his return. I awaited with not a little going on in my mind. Was it excitement or perhaps just plain worry?

During his two weeks of absence, I caused the house to be cleaned from top to bottom. There was much soot to remove from the walls, caused by the use of candles and coal on the fires over the years. Sir John had suggested that I took an easier position on how much of the work I did, and it be true we had a good number of staff. I felt at this stage I must show an example to the others. I believe that my ideas worked, for never were there any complaints made to me. I did receive requests as be proper, for such things as would be deemed necessary for the running of the house, and such like for the animals. For this either Peter or Thomas obliged me and ran errands for all manner of things for the house.

Soon Sarah came to me.

'Mistress Bet, what would you like me to do, now that the cleaning be finished?'

'See to the fires in the five rooms, and keep Sir John's bed aired with the bed pan. Dust the rooms for you know how quickly the dust settles here. So do these things every day.'

The whole house be of a clean and tidy state after ten busy days. This meant I'm left on my own with near idle hands, for which I have but little remedy. Too much time to brood and worry; stood by the window in the front room. Hidden inside me is still that poor girl, who with beating heart awaits the sound of Sir John's coach still days away.

The two weeks turned out to be thirteen days. They be long days indeed, and we were not unready for Sir John when he arrived, because Miss Grimshaw had just that morning cooked a large bake. This consisted of various cakes, pies and tarts. I made my cheese and onion pie, most unusual for a head housekeeper, I know. But Miss Grimshaw be well aware that I have no shrift with convention in this sense. And all this be the favourite fare of the good Sir. His rooms are aired, as be his bed, ready for him should he be tired and needed to retire early.

Eventually the time came and Sir John's coach arrived at about two of the clock. I couldn't but help myself as I moved towards his arms upon his return. But this was a public place and propriety must be observed, so he kissed me upon the cheek, and as he held me by my shoulders he said quietly, so only I could hear, 'My dear Bet, we'll talk later,' He looked at me, smiled and turned away to organize the luggage.

I understood perfectly for indeed our behaviour must be proper. But 'tis no cure, nor help, for my breast which heaved and where inside a loving heart beat so, and I knew I must wait until later, when I be able to converse privately with Sir John. Tis by good chance Francis the dressmaker had arrived earlier that day and delivered my completed new clothing ready to try on. My expectations had built up over two previous visits. The fittings, whose degree of pleasure be new to me, perchance be not difficult to imagine. My Mother never had a stitch of new clothing in her life.

'I must see you wearing your new dress and coat,' said Sir John after his chests were delivered by Peter and Thomas to his room.

I took the dressmaker into the anteroom, so excited be I, while she beamed with pleasure.

'You will soon look so grand in these I'm sure, for you have the most perfect figure. I cannot but wait to see,' she said, as she unwrapped the tissue from around two parcels of clothes.

With her help I did dress with a certain care and learning, for being the first time in clothes, made so fine, I could but hardly believe, while I showed some wonder with the many buttons which had all to be fastened. Francis had much tolerance of my ignorance of such things as she educated me on how to arrange my dress. While she be happy that I understood her instruction; she shocked me as if by some foreign means, the likes of which dug to my very core; a simple statement by someone with no reason to lie.

'You be of most uncommon beauty Miss Bet. Oh, how I envy you for Sir John must only feel to be the luckiest man alive.' She stared at me and stated he had spent a goodly amount on these clothes.

This did bring tears to my eyes. How could a bastard by birth be envied by anyone? Surely not. I quickly blinked the tears away, being happy with my natural reflection in the glass, (for apart from a little foundation cream given to me by Miss Grimshaw I rely upon my natural look.) I dashed, as be impossible for me to do otherwise, to the sitting room where Sir John waited patiently, stood afore the window. I with some reason now felt proud of how I looked. I wondered if this be correct for a young woman to feel so?

'The light blue dress so befits you,' he murmured, 'for like a Queen you are. And the overcoat in dark blue; please turn around, yes! How do you feel Bet, are they comfortable?' He asked?

I must have sounded like an excited child, 'Oh Sir John, they fit with perfection.'

A smile beamed across his face.

Later in the family room when we were finally alone together, he was able to talk for the first time since his return. 'My dear Bet, I have missed you so, you cannot know how much.'

He put his arms around me and pulled me in close. I felt a little uncomfortable.

'John, I do believe I know, for I feel so too. For indeed it has been a miserable time for me waiting here. I have occupied myself and kept the staff busy. Every room has been cleaned and aired out. I swear I should have gone mad without the occupation of my mind, so much do I think of you,' At this point he spoke out.

'My Dear Bet, you have no need to tell me for I can see the house is cleaned and polished. This I noticed when I walked in through the door.'

He is unshaven but I care not as we kiss. I can sense he wants more, and I feel panic as I break away from him.

Later as we enjoy afternoon tea together, Sir John had a thought and placed his china cup and saucer down on the side table.

'Bet I have a confession to make.'

I had a moment to wonder what this could be as Sir John gathered his thoughts.

'From an early age I enjoyed sailing in Jamaica, and I do miss it. So dear Bet, I want you to come with me to Southampton. I may purchase a small yacht and perchance something else. What say you, would you like to accompany me?'

I had but a scant idea where Southampton be, though tis true I would follow Sir John anywhere.

'Of course, I'll come,' I answered without a thought and wondered so as to his intentions.

'In the meantime, I have this pile of papers to see to and file away before we go tomorrow.'

I took my leave of Sir John and made my way along the corridor back to my room. I still wore the new dress and did take much care to pack it into my trunk, used for travelling, which Sir John had seen fit to give me. Into this large chest my possessions fitted with ease. I no longer looked like a scullery maid and was fortunate to be also now possessed of good shoes and items necessary for the comfort and status of a head housekeeper about to travel.

I arose at the normal time of six o'clock, and was quite surprised to find that Sir John awaited me at his breakfast table. He indicated a place laid out for me. I started the day with such a surprise.

'Oh John, why have you laid out a place for me?' I found it hard to overcome my surprise nay shock, for the likes of me to be waited upon by Sir John; that he could be so thoughtful.

'Bet, my dear Bet, this be such a small thing, and it will give me pleasure for you to join me. I've organized breakfast for us together as a surprise.' First, he kissed me on the cheek, then took my hand as he escorted me to the table.

I did truly feel like a lady, and warm emotions rose as I asked myself was I worthy of his kindness?

During breakfast I expressed a concern about the running of the house while we were away.

'I've had a word with Thomas, and he was most pleased that I asked him. He expressed a desire to do anything I asked, and told me that the house would be well run in my absence.'

There was much to talk about, but we had no time. Our journey which awaited us I believed to be long and arduous.

'Let's get started,' said Sir John.

I was already dressed in suitable clothes with my chest packed. Sir John was also ready. Thomas and Peter loaded up the coach and roped our chests down. Thomas checked everything then he gave me a wink, and one of his wide smiles. I noticed and nodded towards him as if to understand, but I didn't, and this troubled me in no small way. What could he mean I did but wonder? I still worried myself as the coach rocked and the horse's harness creaked and jangled as the leather stretched, all with a Ro-hoe and a crack of the whip, which set the horses in motion, as we left Colesdale Hall. Some hours later we arrived at York, and had our luggage loaded aboard the coach headed for Bristol where we bid good bye to the two brothers.

To the end of England we headed, and I felt on the occasion

that Sir John wanted to converse with me, but with four other persons who shared the cab he couldn't. What a bumpy shaking ride it was, and the dust covered us by the end of the day. A lady who sat next to me was a dear, so advanced in age and yet she travelled to Bristol to help her daughter in childbirth for the fourth time. We stopped overnight in Bristol at a Flying Duck Inn where we stayed in dormitories. My fortune was to spend the night on a straw mattress in moderate comfort with five ladies of varied class in one room. Without regret we left next morning and made our way slowly onwards to Southampton.

We arrived at the outskirts of Southampton in the early evening, and I found a pleasant room already booked for my comfort and enjoyment.

Chapter Thirty Three: A moment I'll never forget

The next morn after a hearty breakfast we boarded a hired carriage. How wonderful to ride now in well sprung comfort with the scenery to enjoy; after a journey of but a few minutes across Southampton we started to climb up a long, long hill of perhaps a mile in length, from which at one point we overlooked the port which led us well into the countryside. We passed a small farm which Sir John indicated to me; the significance of which I only understood later. We travelled for but a minute or two then he bid the coachman stop. He halted the stallion, jumped down then unfolded the two steps and helped me down with perfect courtesy. We were presented with the sight of a large attractive though overgrown house set back from the road, with several outbuildings which stretched out behind.

'Pray wait! We will be some fifteen minutes,' said Sir John to the coachman.

I remember well my first impression was of shock as I realised this could not be a social call, for who would be able to live in a house so overgrown. I was somewhat slow today.

He spoke to me, 'Please come with me. I have the keys, and I want you to see inside. This house has been empty for some time.'

Dumbfounded, I followed Sir John as we made our way past overgrown trees, rhododendron bushes and rampant weeds to the four stone steps which led up to the front door. After several tries, it eventually gave way and the lock turned, 'Just needs a little lamp oil. You'll see,' said Sir John as he pushed hard, the door finally opened with a loud dry creek, a sound louder than any frog could produce.

This property is for sale,' he said as he led the way.

My mind was in a whirl, unable to think. For Sale, so he wants to buy it?

The interior is a little dusty but well furnished, and look at the size of these rooms,' he continued.

'Bet, it be my wish to make this our first home if you agree.'

This be something I could never dream he would ask me and I hesitated as I tried to answer him. I believe I did try.

'John we are friends,' I start to worry for but one moment, as my birth-right threatens to haunt me. So, I show him my ring as a reminder which he gave me those two long years ago.

'Come on! There be more to see, Follow me!'

He had turned my thoughts away from that dark area deep inside my head. And I was like an excited child as he led the way and charged through the house with no need to drag me. I be near to overwhelmed by all this, as we scamper around and through more rooms than I were able to count.

'Do you like it?' he eventually asked me.

My head was still in a spin as I took in his question.

'With a fair amount of work this will make a fine residence,' I managed to say. My mind raced faster than a horse. We were in one of the front rooms looking out of a bay window where the shutters had been opened. We stood side by side and spoke about what could be done with the large area and how a lawn could easily be cultivated and how nice it would be. Sir John had been quiet for a few seconds and I turned to discover why. I became aware that he had dropped to one knee. I looked on in wonder; no doubt my jaw had dropped too.

'I have here this engagement ring that used to belong to my grandmother, and is dear to my heart; I want you to wear it. Betty May, will you marry me?'

This was the easiest question he asked me that day, and required no thought.

'Yes, of course I will.'

He held my left hand and slid the ring down my middle finger. I could never have imagined a more wonderful feeling.

'Bet you have made me a happy man, for you light up my life. You will want for nothing for I'm a wealthy man. I promise you this, I want to do more good in this world. I will tell you the full story of my life, for why I was knighted and of my time in Jamaica, at a more appropriate time and place.

With both of us locked arm in arm, we chatted happily together and made our way back to the coach where the two horses and driver waited patiently for us.

'To the docks cabbie, I have a boat to look at,' instructed Sir John.

This was where my diary marked the end of, 'My First Life,' and the beginning of my second. I feel that much is to be expected of me now and do hope that The Lord sees fit to favour me that I may serve Sir John to the best of my abilities and as circumstances see fit.

I look at my precious diary and realise there are still many pages yet to fill. A little like my life. So, now I start 'My Second Life' on a new page.

END

About the Author

Melvyn Lumb is a writer who realised late in his life a love for writing. Betty May is his first novel and stems from his short story, 'A Dog's Dinner.' He has won several competitions on Fanstory, a writer's site. His entry 'A Nagasaki boy,' won a flash fiction story of the month award. A sequel to Betty May is planned. . .

Printed in Great Britain
by Amazon

21269106R00149